King Arthur

OTHER OXFORD CLASSIC TALES

One Thousand and One Arabian Nights
Retold by Geraldine McCaughrean

Moby Dick
Retold by Geraldine McCaughrean

El Cid
Retold by Geraldine McCaughrean

Gulliver's Travels
Retold by James Riordan

Don Quixote
Retold by Michael Harrison

King Arthur

Retold by James Riordan

Illustrated by Rosamund Fowler

OXFORD
UNIVERSITY PRESS

OXFORD
UNIVERSITY PRESS

Great Clarendon Street, Oxford OX2 6DP

Oxford University Press is a department of the University of Oxford.
It furthers the University's objective of excellence in research, scholarship,
and education by publishing worldwide in

Oxford New York

Athens Auckland Bangkok Bogotá Buenos Aires
Cape Town Chennai Dar es Salaam Delhi Florence Hong Kong Istanbul
Karachi Kolkata Kuala Lumpur Madrid Melbourne Mexico City Mumbai
Nairobi Paris São Paulo Shanghai Singapore Taipei Tokyo Toronto Warsaw

with associated companies in Berlin Ibadan

Oxford is a registered trade mark of Oxford University Press
in the UK and in certain other countries

British Library Cataloguing in Publication Data available

ISBN 0 19 274194 2

1 3 5 7 9 10 8 6 4 2

Typeset by AFS Image Setters Ltd, Glasgow

Printed in Great Britain by
Cox & Wyman Ltd, Reading, Berkshire

Contents

Prologue

He clung to the edge of the sky like a tear in the eye of the storm. Then he was falling and darkness enclosed him, wrapping him firmly in its folds. Only the bright glow of a sword, held out before him like a torch, lit up his path. The path that was no path, the goal that was unknown.

Dimly, the sense of his father's thoughts echoed in his mind: 'You, my son, must avenge my death.'

Then there was the falling, the darkness, and the silence. And then ahead he gradually made out a distant break in the gloom, as though someone had stuck a pin through the great velvet pall and let in a glimmer of light.

Sounds began to fill his head and with them came words. He was standing on something called 'sand', he heard 'waves' strike a 'shore', he felt a wet 'spray' touch his face and 'splash' against the sea—'rain' someone called it.

His other senses followed in swift succession. Smell

1

came first and with it the tang of salt air and a fresh fragrance he associated at once with greenness and growth. Then touch. His fingers were clutching a reassuring hand; he hung on as if his life depended on it.

A sadness overtook him, a sense of loss.

Somewhere he became aware of a warm voice that spoke out of the mist, 'Come, sleep. You are safe now. Let us dream together.'

At once he knew peace, such peace as he had never known in all his two years upon the earth. After never-ending wakefulness he could sleep at last. And dream.

In his dream he saw again the sword that had flashed in the heavens before spiralling downwards, vanishing without a splash into a dark pool of water.

Thus began his dream which was to encompass four centuries. Events passed before him in alternating light and dark—the coming of the Romans, their soldiers stationed in hilltop forts and camps. He saw a peaceful country crisscrossed with roads that joined towns and villages; there were farmers growing corn, raising cattle, and moving crops to market in horse-drawn wagons. There were harbours and lighthouses round the coasts; swimming baths and theatres in the towns; and tribes of Britons, all with their own kings, living under Roman rule.

Then the last Roman legions left the land and raiders crossed the seas to burn and kill and occupy the land. Once more the country was split into warring tribes, and the suffering people longed for a strong king who might unite the land.

In his dream he heard the names of Uther Pendragon, his father; of Merlin, his father's bard whom some called a wizard; even of Arthur—his own name; of his mother

Igraine; and of her daughter, his half-sister, Morgana Le Fay, who cursed him for stealing her birthright. He stirred restlessly in his dream, as if sensing the hatred that burned in her breast, the revenge she was planning as she studied the black arts.

The dream had now turned into a nightmare. In a fever, he glimpsed broken scenes—of his dying father— poisoned by the black-hearted Vortigern; of flight in Merlin's arms down a secret path under cover of darkness; of the waiting skiff and dangerous sea journey round Land's End to the mysterious valleys of Powys; of their refuge in a cave beside the River Towy, near Carmarthen.

He clearly saw the Red Dragon flag fluttering over what were once his father's lands—the hated blood-red emblem of Vortigern.

Yet through his dream came Merlin's words:

'One day, Arthur, you will be king. You will unite this troubled land.'

That gave him comfort as he lay, between waking and sleeping, in the arms of the earth, listening for voices of others whose song he would one day join.

1

The Red and White Dragons

While Arthur was growing up and learning skills and magic from Merlin, his tutor, the evil Vortigern was plotting with two German tribes, the English and the Saxons—known as the Anglo-Saxons. Vortigern had invited them to settle in Britain: to help him in his fight against the Britons and other tribes.

In the passing of time, however, the barbarian invaders wanted the islands for themselves. And, having grown strong and driven the Britons back, they turned on Vortigern—for he had outlived his usefulness.

In fear of his life, Vortigern summoned his counsellors. What was he to do? They told him plainly, 'Take your army to the farthermost corner of the land and build a fortress strong enough to withstand assault. For your enemies will seek to kill you and occupy your lands.'

So Vortigern fled with his followers, making for the mountains of North Wales. There he found a site in the mountains; a tall rocky crag seemed an impregnable stronghold against the Anglo-Saxons.

Yet when his workmen had assembled stones and timber for the fortress, a strange thing happened. As they went to lay the foundations, they found their work constantly reduced to ruins. No matter how well they sealed the base in the mountain rock, water seeped through each night and flooded the site.

So it continued, night after night. At last Vortigern's patience gave out and he flew into a rage. Summoning his counsellors once more, he cried, 'What is the meaning of this? There must be magic in the air. Tell me what must be done or I'll have you all boiled in oil!'

The men studied the stars, picked through the entrails of a sheep, and debated the past night's dreams. Finally, they came to Vortigern with their decision.

'This is magic ground, my lord. The *tuatha de danaan*—spirits of the goddess Danu—are angry and demand a sacrifice. You must sprinkle the earth with the blood of a fatherless prince. Only then can the fortress be built.'

Vortigern rubbed his chin. Where was he to find such a prince?

At once he sent messengers to search. And, as the weeks turned into months, a band of his soldiers rode into Carmarthen.

Now, although Merlin was able to instruct Arthur in the mysteries of his magic books, it was not enough. The boy needed archers, horsemen, and swordsmen to teach him fighting skills. The young Arthur also longed for games with children of his own age. So now and then Merlin took the curly-haired twelve-year-old into Carmarthen where the lively boy could play and learn the arts of knighthood.

It so happened, therefore, as one of Vortigern's men

was watching a game of football, he chanced to overhear one boy shout at another, 'You tripped me! I shall tell your father.'

At that the other boy—a tall, gangling lad—laughed, saying, 'My father was once a mighty king, but now he is dead.'

When the game had ended, Arthur made his way home to the cave above the River Towy. He did not notice soldiers following at a distance. After he had disappeared into the cave, the soldiers crept up to the entrance in the rock and peered inside. They had a dreadful fright.

For inside sat a cobwebby figure, sitting still in meditation, as if encrusted in the mossy stone. His long white hair and beard seemed frosted over, trapped by the steady drip of time.

Had the boy changed by magic into this old fossil?

As they watched in awe, the man's dim sea-blue eyes opened, he sighed, shivered, and stretched out a trembling, deathly-white hand towards the men. 'Whissstt,' he hissed. 'What is it that you want?'

An officer stepped nervously forward, asking, 'Where is the boy?'

At that, Arthur himself appeared from the depths of the cave. Before he could speak, a hail of questions met him:

'What is your name? Who is your father? Where is your mother? Do you have royal blood?'

Merlin cut the officer short.

'Any answers we give will be to your lord alone. But first we must know the meaning of the questions.'

'Our king, Vortigern, has heard of a wise young boy hereabouts. He wishes to seek his advice. You see, only a fatherless prince can help him build his fortress on Mount Eryri.'

Merlin knew the truth—that they wanted Arthur's blood. But he held his tongue. To Arthur he whispered, 'This is our chance to take revenge on the evil Vortigern. Let us go with the men.'

Arthur addressed the soldiers, 'Take me to your king and we shall see if my advice holds true.'

With Merlin and Arthur astride one horse, and two soldiers sharing another, the band of men set off for Vortigern's camp. Although they rode hard throughout the daylight hours, the journey took three full days before they sighted the snow-capped mountains.

High on a crag Arthur could make out the ruins of a half-built fortress: the white stone walls had cracked and crumbled, the flagpole bearing the red dragon flag had snapped in two and the flag lay crumpled on the ground. A reek of decay filled the air.

As they rode through a village of tents, Arthur noticed the hunched figures of men and women, and the pinched, starving faces of little children. Clearly, this ragbag of camp-followers was all that remained of Vortigern's once-mighty army.

What surprised Arthur were the curious, even pitying stares he was getting from the crowd. What could that mean?

Riding up to a large pavilion, the men dismounted and ushered the old man and boy inside. Vortigern was lounging on a couch, surrounded by his attendants.

'Welcome to my domain,' he said with an attempt at a reassuring smile. 'It is only a temporary field-camp while my new palace is being built.'

Turning to Arthur, he said, 'I've brought you here, lad, to seek your help. My counsellors say you might be of use to me.'

At that he winked to his men.

'Why me?' asked Arthur. 'Are your wise men too ignorant to advise you?'

'Sometimes a beardless boy is wiser than a star-gazer,' replied the king sourly.

'Does the great and powerful Vortigern rely on a beardless boy for wisdom?' asked Arthur boldly.

Vortigern's eyes blazed. 'Well, if you must know,' he snarled, 'I need your blood, not your brains. Your death will appease the *tuatha de danaan*.'

'You are as stupid as you are cruel, Vortigern,' broke in Merlin. 'Down the ages kings and priests have sacrificed humans to the gods. But it never did any good. Nor will it now.'

Arthur added, 'Kill me, drench the soil with my blood—it will only add to the flood. Ask your wise men what lies beneath the mountain. Then you might discover what is ruining the work.'

Vortigern bristled at the boy's insolence. But he held his tongue, wondering how he might employ him best. To himself he muttered, 'If this pipsqueak is so clever, let him tell me what to do—I can always dispose of him later, along with the whitebeard.'

So he summoned his counsellors to the tent.

Meanwhile, Arthur and Merlin whispered together for several minutes. Then the boy stepped forward and asked the wise men, 'Tell me, what lies beneath the fortress foundations?'

The men admitted, 'We do not know.'

'Then I will tell you,' said Arthur. 'Command the workmen to dig deep, and they will find an underground lake. Let them remove the earth's canopy from the lake and drain the waters.'

Arthur paused as the men shifted uneasily; then he asked, 'Tell me, what is in the lake?'

The counsellors kept silent, shrugging their shoulders.

'I will tell you,' said Arthur. 'On the lake-bed you will find two great stone urns.'

The men were puzzled.

'Tell me,' continued Arthur, 'what is inside the urns?'

Again the men were silent. 'I will tell you. Inside each urn is a folded cloth. And do you know what is inside the cloth?'

They shook their heads.

'Then I will tell you. Inside the cloths are two sleeping dragons—one white, one red.'

At that the counsellors looked at Vortigern as if to say: 'What nonsense this boy speaks!'

But Arthur smiled knowingly, saying, 'The rest you will discover for yourselves. But be assured: the fortress will then stand tall and strong.'

Vortigern was uncertain what to believe. But there was nothing to lose by following the boy's advice.

'Right, lad, show my masons where to dig,' he said. 'If what you say is true, I shall spare your life. If not, you and the old man will be the foundation stones of my new palace.'

Soon the picks and hammers of a hundred men rang round the mountainside. They broke up the rock, dug out the soil and sent clods and stones rolling down the hill. Hours passed before someone gave a weary shout, 'We've broken through!'

The diggers all crowded round, peering through the hole into the gaping void below. There beneath the ground was the dark shimmering surface of a lake.

It took the men three days to clear the earthy crust

9

above the sheet of water. Then the engineers took over, pumping out the clear waters of the lake and sending them tumbling down the mountain in a swirling stream to the valley below.

When all the water was drained, the men spied two strange stone urns standing in the bowl of cracked grey mud.

Just then a noise like a thunderclap rose from the lake-bed and the two urns started to crack like giant eggs, revealing two folded cloths. From the cloths emerged scaly claws and limbs; shiny forked tongues flicked out as if testing the air; then balls of fire billowed through the mist.

Within moments two dragons had crawled out: one white, one red. Both were breathing fire that hissed and fizzled in the damp air. On seeing each other, they let out a roar and crouched down ready to spring, snorting gusts of purple smoke and orange flame.

Then all was a tangled mass of tearing claws and jaws, flailing tails and beating feet. Soon the White Dragon had the other down and was ripping at its throat. The dying dragon's tail thrashed wildly in the mud until, with a fearful shudder, it lay stone dead upon its back, oozing jagged streams of blood.

With a roar of triumph, the White Dragon beat its wings like crashing cymbals and rose into the sky. It climbed up and over the mountain, then wheeled away, panting fire, towards the sun.

In the silence that ensued, Merlin's voice rang out like a tolling bell: 'The prophecy is coming true.'

His blue eyes turned ruby red.

The watching Vortigern was stunned, his mouth gaping as he stared into the sky. Finally, he turned to

Arthur and asked in a trembling voice, 'What does all this mean?'

'You will not welcome the truth,' said Arthur.

'But I must know.'

'Very well, then. This lake represents the world,' explained the boy. 'The urn and cloth with the White Dragon inside are Britain; those with the Red Dragon are the invaders. When the White Dragon rises up and slays the Red, that is the British driving out their foes and the traitors who sided with them. Then the prophecy will come true.'

'But what prophecy?' Vortigern asked.

Arthur spoke loudly for all to hear:

> 'When dragons fight, and White slays Red,
> The time is come; the foe has fled;
> Britons arise, peace to bring,
> For Arthur is the true-born king!'

Vortigern's deep voice cracked with fear as he asked further, 'But who are you? How do you know what is to come? And who is this Arthur, the true-born king?'

The boy smiled to Merlin before declaring, 'I am Arthur, son of Uther Pendragon, the king you poisoned and whose crown you stole. You, Vortigern, are a traitor to your people. You brought in the Anglo-Saxons to fight your battles; and you run away when they turn on you. You have brought nothing but war and misery to our land.'

Merlin stepped forward and took Arthur's arm, pointing a bony finger at the trembling Vortigern.

'It is I, Merlin, Pendragon's bard, who taught Arthur the secrets of the Sight. All he says is true. Go, now, while there is still time. Leave these shores, never to return!'

11

After all he had witnessed, Vortigern knew that his only chance was to do as Merlin said. He did not wish to share the Red Dragon's fate.

Taking a few trusted soldiers, he rode out of Wales and was never seen again.

Some say he died soon after in a castle which the Saxons burnt to the ground. Others say he escaped to the other side of the world and settled in what is now called Patagonia.

As for Arthur and Merlin, they returned to the cave near Carmarthen.

'Back to your studies, Arthur,' said Merlin sternly. 'You still have much to learn if you are to be the greatest king this land will ever see.'

A frown clouded the boy's freckled face, and he swallowed a sigh before sitting down before his musty books, Merlin's astrolabe and crystal ball.

It was much more fun playing football.

2

Arthur Becomes King

F our more years passed in learning the knightly arts. By now Arthur was a tall, broad-shouldered youth of sixteen, with flowing dark hair down to his shoulders and eyes of sparkling grey. A sprinkling of spring freckles on his nose betrayed his boyhood; yet his quick determined step marked the budding assurance of the man. No youth could match him in wrestling, fencing, archery, or any other sport.

Arthur was now spending much of his time with a young Welsh nobleman, Sir Kay, who was four years older than himself. Kay had been made knight at All Hallowmass the year before. He was the only son of Sir Hector who owned estates in many parts of Wales; with Merlin's blessing, he and his wife had become like father and mother to young Arthur these past few years.

With Uther and Vortigern gone, the realm had collapsed into many feuding estates, with every baron, however low or mighty, bidding to be lord of his domain and striving to extend his power.

One day, Merlin went to London to visit the archbishop, advising him to summon all the lords of the realm and gentlemen-at-arms.

'Have them gather at the abbey church on Christmas Day,' said Merlin. 'It is time to unite Britain under a single king. On the holy day of Christmas the lords will witness a miracle and learn who is to be the rightful king.'

Now the archbishop greatly respected Merlin's wisdom, and sent for all the lords of the realm, bidding them come to London at Christmas. Thus it was that lords and ladies arrived at the abbey church for the Christmas morning service.

After matins, the noble lords strolled out of the church, arm-in-arm with their fair ladies; but they were in for a shock. For there in the churchyard was a marble block where none had stood before. And stuck fast by the point inside the marble was a mighty sword. As the lords and ladies crowded round, they read letters of gold carved in the stone:

WHOSOEVER DRAWS THIS SWORD
IS THE RIGHTFUL
KING OF ENGLAND

Many a noble lord aspired to be king, so there was certainly no lack of volunteers. Each pushed forward to try his luck; yet however hard they pulled and pushed, none could as much as move the sword.

It was stuck fast.

'He who is destined to be king is evidently not here,' said the archbishop. 'But God will no doubt make him known to us when the time is right. My noble lords, I bid you gather here on New Year's Day, following the

14

tournament. Then whoever wishes may try the sword again.'

Now every year, on New Year's Day, a grand jousting tournament was held upon the meadows at Westminster. Knights came from every corner of the land—and from far-flung countries overseas—to joust and test their sword and archery skills.

The sword in the stone attracted greater crowds than ever before, and on New Year's Day the fields were teeming with flags and banners, jostling piemen, and colourful jesters—and, of course, a host of gallant knights on horseback and on foot, all in shining armour. Their ladies paraded in flowing gowns and warm cloaks to protect them from the biting winds.

Among the knights who had come to London were Sir Hector and his son Sir Kay: they had ridden from Carmarthen to test their skills at the tournament; and they had brought young Arthur to help with the mounts and armour. Having lodged overnight at a house nearby, they were riding to the jousting fields early on New Year's Day when Sir Kay suddenly missed his sword.

'Arthur, pray go and fetch it,' he said.

Arthur willingly rode back to the lodgings, but found the house locked and no one home—everyone had left for the tournament. Arthur was keen to help his friend: Sir Kay must have a sword or he could not enter the lists and be admitted to the tournament. All at once, Arthur recalled the sword he had seen in the abbey churchyard the day before.

No one had told him of the inscription on the stone.

If he had known he might have realized that the sword was meant for him. After all, he knew from Merlin that one day he was destined to be king. For the moment, however, his one thought was to do his duty by his friend.

What if I ride to the churchyard and borrow that sword in the stone? he thought. Maybe I can put it back later before it is missed.

Riding to the abbey yard, he dismounted, strode over to the stone and placed his hand upon the hilt. No one was around since all were at the jousts. With barely an effort, he pulled it out of the marble block. He was in such a hurry he did not stop to read the words of gold. Hastening back to Sir Kay, he thrust the sword into his hand.

The moment the young knight set eyes on the gleaming sword, he realized what it was. With a cry of joy, he rode over to his father, shouting, 'Father, look, look, here is the sword from the stone. It must be me! I must be the rightful king!'

When Sir Hector saw the sword, he recognized it at once. But he was unsure about his son.

'How did you come by the sword,' he asked, knowing the young man had been with him all the while.

'It is mine, I tell you,' cried Sir Kay. 'I am the rightful king.'

Arthur kept silent.

'Come,' said Sir Hector. 'Follow me.'

Sir Hector rode to the abbey church, with Sir Kay and Arthur following on behind. Once at the church, all three dismounted and passed through the doorway. The two young men trailed behind Sir Hector as he strode purposefully to the altar. There he stopped before an open Bible.

'Here,' he said to his son, 'swear on the holy Bible how you came by the sword.'

Reluctantly placing his right hand upon the open book, Sir Kay confessed, 'Sir, Arthur brought it to me.'

'But how did *you* obtain the sword!' asked Sir Hector, turning to Arthur.

'I will tell you, sir,' said Arthur, blushing. 'When I rode to our lodgings for Sir Kay's sword, I found no one home. Rather than return empty-handed, I came here and pulled this sword from the stone. I swear I meant to put it back after the tournament—'

'Did anyone see you?' broke in Sir Hector.

'I do not think so.'

Sir Hector gazed fondly into the honest face of the young man.

'Do you realize what this means?' he said. 'If what you say is true, you are to be King of England.'

Although Arthur knew all about his destiny, even so it came now as quite a shock. 'So soon! By whose wish?' was all he could say.

'By the will of God,' replied Sir Hector. 'Whosoever draws the sword is the rightful king of England. Now, show me if you can draw it out again—so there can be no doubt.'

Putting the sword back into the marble stone, Arthur stood aside as first Sir Hector, then Sir Kay tried to withdraw it. They failed.

'Now you try,' said Sir Hector to Arthur.

The boy stepped forward and pulled it out as easily as a knife from butter. As he turned round, the heavy sword in his hand, he was surprised to see the two men, father and son, kneeling at his feet.

'If it is God's will that I be king,' Arthur said with a sigh, 'I shall not fail you. You have been like father and brother to me.'

'All I ask,' said Sir Hector, 'is that you make my son your steward when you are king.'

'So be it,' said Arthur. 'For as long as he and I both live, Sir Kay alone shall be my steward.'

Thereupon, Sir Hector led Arthur to the archbishop and related how Arthur had pulled the sword out of the stone.

The archbishop stared uncertainly at the young man: he seemed far too youthful to be king of Britain.

'We must be absolutely sure,' the archbishop said. 'For there will be doubters. Let all the barons come here on the Twelfth Day after Christmas; then once more we will have a sword-pulling test.'

So Arthur put back the sword into the stone. From then on it was guarded day and night by ten noble knights, right up to the Twelfth Day after Christmas. Many then came forward; when all had failed, the archbishop beckoned Arthur forward.

The lad stepped towards the stone and, as the huge crowd watched in hushed silence, he pulled out the sword with ease.

An awed silence descended on the barons. In truth, they were furious. They thought it shameful for the realm to be ruled by a mere boy of unknown parents. At their insistence a final decision was put off to Candlemas, when all the barons would assemble again.

At Candlemas even more lords arrived from near and far to try their luck. But none could shift the sword. And just as Arthur did on the Twelfth Day, so he did at Candlemas, pulling out the sword with ease.

Still the barons were not content. Another trial was set for the high feast of Easter. Again, as Arthur did at Candlemas, so he did at Easter. But the barons still refused to make him king.

And a new test was set for Pentecost, which we now call Whitsun. Again, Arthur alone could extract the sword—to the fury of the barons. Prompted by Merlin, however, the archbishop now called a halt. For a great crowd had gathered and the mood was growing ugly against the lords. People were shouting Arthur's name and cursing the barons.

'Arthur, Arthur! Long live the king! It is God's will. Down with those against him. Long live the king! Arthur, Arthur, Arthur, God save King Arthur!'

As the host of men, women, and children fell to their knees, the noble lords and ladies slowly did the same, the rich beside the poor, bowing their heads and begging mercy for their doubts.

Arthur readily forgave them all, held the sword high in both hands, then passed into the abbey and laid it on the altar. The archbishop received the gift gratefully and at once accepted Arthur into the holy order of knighthood.

At his coronation, which swiftly followed, Arthur took the vow which once his father had solemnly made:

'I swear to both lords and commoners to be a true king, to stand for justice at all times, and to serve my country from now and through all my days.'

Then King Arthur summoned all the noble lords to swear allegiance to the crown. He invited anyone to complain freely of any wrongs done to them since the death of his father, King Uther Pendragon. Those who had lost land had it returned; those who had stolen land were punished.

Once this was done, King Arthur assembled all the armies of the realm, led by the best of the older knights who had served his father, and of younger knights eager to show courage and loyalty to the new king. Then, with this great army behind him, he set out to strengthen his rule in all the counties of England up to the River Trent, driving back the Saxons and punishing all traitors who had taken the enemy side. Before long he had brought peace and order to the whole of southern Britain, and made his capital at Camelot, which we now call Winchester.

But not everyone accepted his rule. Those whose power covered the north of England, Scotland, Ireland, and Wales were suspicious of the beardless boy who called himself the rightful king of Britain.

So Arthur, on Merlin's advice, sent messengers into their territories, seeking a meeting at Pentecost with the rebellious kings; the meeting place was to be in the city of Caerleon in South Wales. Arthur awaited their arrival at Caerleon Castle high on a hill. He soon had news that eleven kings with eleven thousand men were marching on the town. Among them were King Lot of Lothian, King Agwisance of Ireland, King Carados of Scotland, King Clarvus of Northumberland, even King Idres of Cornwall who had joined the rebel side.

Believing they were coming in peace, Arthur sent rich gifts to the kings; but they sent back sharp replies: they, too, had gifts—a sword between Arthur's neck and shoulders, a lance between his ribs!

Since his five hundred men would hardly withstand their eleven thousand, Arthur retreated into the castle and barricaded it against the foe. And when the mighty armies laid siege they were unable to capture the king.

After fifteen days, with food and water running low, Merlin appeared on the castle ramparts, his arms held high. In the ensuing hush, Merlin addressed the hostile kings and knights.

'Lay down your arms and listen to what I have to say,' he shouted to the armies. 'When I have finished, make your own judgement on the king.

'Arthur is the rightful king of Britain. Not just of the land up to the Trent, but of Wales and Scotland, Ireland and the Orkneys. One day he will rule other countries too.

'After the death of his father, King Uther Pendragon, I took him secretly to the valleys of South Wales and schooled him in wisdom and chivalry, preparing him for the throne. Three special gifts I gave him: to be the bravest and most just of kings; to be the greatest king this land will ever know; and to rule longer than any king before.

'Soon he shall own a sword, Excalibur, which even now is being forged by magic in the Vale of Avalon. With that sword he will lead you to your greatest glories, driving out the Saxons and uniting this great land. Kneel before him now, he is your king!'

As Merlin finished speaking, Arthur emerged to stand beside him on the ramparts. Silence descended on the hostile kings; many felt that a time of greatness was indeed at hand. A murmur spread through row upon row of soldiers, knights, and kings. And one by one they knelt and bowed their heads. The murmur grew into cheers and jubilation.

The archbishop now appeared on the ramparts; once more he placed the crown on Arthur's head and raised his hand in blessing. As Arthur prepared to speak, a hush spread through the ranks of men below.

'Tomorrow we march to the north, west, and east; together we shall drive our enemies out of Britain. Together we will build fortresses and look-out towers all round our coasts to warn us of invasion. Together we will rebuild the towns and churches the barbarians have destroyed; we will lay new roads so that our knights can ride all over Britain to punish those who break the peace.

'Together we will make our country great again.'

So began King Arthur's reign.

3
Excalibur

A sword had brought Arthur to the throne; but he had made a gift of it to the archbishop. One day he mentioned to Merlin that he had no worthy sword.

'How I regret giving up the sword in the stone; it would have served me well in wars ahead.'

'It matters not,' muttered Merlin, shaking his long white beard. 'There was no virtue in that sword. It served its purpose in making you king. Tomorrow we will set out to find you a new sword: it was made especially for you. The sword is called Excalibur. So powerful is it that no one can withstand its power—it cuts through iron and steel as easily as a sickle through hay. With Excalibur you will defeat your enemies and bring peace and freedom to your realm.'

They rode out next day at dawn, travelling for several days before they found themselves in a narrow valley hemmed in by dark green mountains. Finally, they climbed to a narrow pass and looked down upon a rocky bowl formed in the mountains; in it was a great lake.

While the mountains were shrouded in deep purple shadow, the lake's waters gleamed in the pale sunshine; at the lakeside willows whitened, aspens quivered upon a lawn of fresh green grass; lilies bloomed in the shallows and, beyond the lake, Arthur saw through a gap in the hills a mysterious broad plain, half hidden in shafts of slanting light.

Arthur and Merlin rode down the steep slope to the lakeside lawn and gazed into the clear blue waters: the lake was so transparent they could see the sandy bed below.

'This is the Lake of Avalon,' murmured Merlin. 'Beyond it, through the hills, lies the plain of Camlann where one distant day you will fight your final battle. Watch carefully now and observe all that happens.'

As Arthur's keen eyes scanned the still waters, he saw a slender arm, clothed in white silk, holding aloft a shining sword. Then, all at once, he caught a soft voice, calling his name—'Arthur, Arthur, welcome, King Arthur'—and there walking across the water towards him was a woman dressed in a pale blue robe, with a girdle of gold about her waist.

'I am Nimue, the Lady of the Lake,' she said—her voice was like the wind sighing in the trees. 'Your sword, Excalibur, awaits you. I have kept it safe until this moment. Come, climb into this barge and take it.'

Seeing a boat floating beneath a willow, Arthur waded into the water and stepped into it. At once it turned about, its prow pointing to the broad expanse of water and moving across the lake as if rowed by unseen hands. When it reached the centre of the mysterious lake its movement ceased, like a boat becalmed upon a windless sea.

As Arthur wonderingly looked about, he suddenly saw a face beneath him in the water. A fair-haired woman was smiling up at him from beneath the mirror-smooth waters of the lake. Her blonde tresses floated all about her and her slender body shimmered in the water's dancing light. Hers was the arm raised above the lake: now she lifted it high, holding aloft a gleaming sword and silver scabbard studded with precious gems. The sword and scabbard burned brightly like a single flame between the water and blue sky.

Arthur reached out and lifted the sword and scabbard from the water, taking them from the silk-clad arm; and he waved them high above his head as if calling his men to battle. The cold water trickled down his sleeve on to his neck and chest.

He stared in awe at the blue steel blade and the hilt of twisted ivory and gold. As he did so, the barge turned about and floated back to the lakeside where Nimue stood waiting to welcome him with a smile.

'Guard well your sword,' she said, 'for it is made of fairy craft. It is meant for you alone, and it will serve you well. But it must be used only in just cause.

'There is one more condition of my gift. You are young and your rule has just begun; but all kings are mortal and one day even you will die. When that day comes, I will recall Excalibur to my lake. It must return to the waters whence it came—otherwise the spell will be broken and your memory will rust away like any sword.'

At that Nimue walked back across the waters and disappeared into the early morning mist. Arthur was so entranced by her beauty, and so taken with the gift, that he had no words to thank her. While his eyes were fixed on the shadow in the mist, he murmured half to himself,

'She has such a lovely face, who is she, this Lady of the Lake?'

Merlin broke into his musings. 'Nimue is an old friend of mine; she is an even greater wizard than I am; so the magic in the sword is very powerful. I see you are very taken with your gifts. Let me ask you this: which is more precious, the scabbard or the sword?'

Arthur smiled at the question. He did not think twice.

'Why, the sword, of course! The scabbard is the most exquisite I have ever seen. But a simple leather sheath would suffice to hold the sword. It is the blade that will do the work.'

'Then you are wrong,' said Merlin gruffly. 'Have you forgotten my teachings so quickly? Things are not always what they seem. In fact, the scabbard is a hundred times more precious than the sword. True, a blade that cuts through the toughest steel is fine indeed. But it is the scabbard that holds the sword and keeps it safe—and preserves your life. As long as you keep the scabbard by your side, you will lose no blood, no matter how hard your enemies strike. Remember this: it is far harder to save a life than take it away.'

In silence Arthur and Merlin rode back to Camelot. Their thoughts were on other things: Merlin's on the lovely Lady of the Lake, Arthur's on his sword and magical scabbard. In the years to come, the destinies of both men were to be entwined with their thoughts on that sunny day.

4

Arthur Marries Guinevere

Within three years of becoming king, Arthur had defeated the Saxons in six great battles; the invaders either fled in their ships or swore allegiance to the king. Thus, peace finally came to all of Britain, and it was to last for many years.

Of course, people still suffered from the evil woven by magicians and witches hiding in forests, from goblins and giants, and from feuds between jealous barons. But the land generally enjoyed a time of peace. And when trouble did break out, King Arthur's knights soon stopped it.

One time, as Arthur was returning from settling just such a dispute, he happened to pass through Camelard, staying overnight at the castle of his father's old friend King Leodegrance.

Now the king had a beautiful daughter, Dame Guinevere; and Arthur fell in love the moment he set eyes on her. Saying nothing to King Leodegrance at the time, he waited until he arrived back at Camelot, and commented casually to Merlin, 'Now that the country is at

peace, perhaps it is right for me to marry. My barons
keep pressing me to take a wife. What do you think?'

Arthur was guided in all matters of importance by
Merlin's wise counsel.

'True, a man of your noble spirit needs a wife,' said
Merlin; 'and the realm surely needs a queen. Tell me, is
there a lady you have in mind or shall I seek a bride for
you?'

With a blush, Arthur confessed, 'I have fallen in love
with Guinevere, daughter of King Leodegrance. She is the
fairest, sweetest, purest, noblest woman in all the world. I
would marry her and no other.'

Merlin stroked his chin thoughtfully and was silent
for a time. How could he tell Arthur what he had seen in
his crystal ball? That one day Guinevere would betray him
and cause his death . . . and the end of a united Britain
too. Merlin was thinking to himself, True, she is very
beautiful; but how I wish he loved another. Her beauty
will bring him down. For a beloved knight of his court
will fall in love with her and bring shame on them all. He
will cause war between Arthur and himself, and enable a
traitor to take the throne . . . Yet there is nothing I can do:
when a man's heart is set on a woman, nothing will
change it.

So at Arthur's bidding, he went to King Leodegrance
and told him that Arthur wished to wed his daughter. The
king was overjoyed.

'Those are the best tidings I have ever had,' he said,
tears running down his cheeks. 'What an honour for so
noble and courageous a king to marry my daughter. Now
what shall I give as dowry? Willingly I would grant him
all my lands and knights, but he has plenty enough
already. I know, I shall send him a gift that will please

him most of all: the Round Table. It was made for his father many years ago; and after his death it was sent to me for safe keeping. Now I shall return it to Uther's son.'

The Round Table could seat one hundred and fifty knights, and had as many carved wooden chairs. It was to be sent in time for the wedding, which was to be at Pentecost.

In the meantime, a few weeks before the wedding, King Arthur held an Easter feast for all the knights at court. Yet as they went to take their seats at the long oak table, each tried to sit nearer the head than the foot—for honour attached to higher places. And scuffles broke out.

Arthur remarked sadly to Merlin, 'Once I am married, none will have cause to fight. There can be no head or foot at a table that is round.'

Arthur asked Merlin to select the most worthy knights to serve at court. And the wise wizard chose only the bravest knights, and brought the archbishop to bless the Round Table and each chair.

On the day of the wedding, the archbishop was present to join the hands of Arthur and Guinevere; and four kings held high their golden swords in a gleaming archway as the happy couple passed out of Saint Stephen's Church at Camelot. When King Arthur and Queen Guinevere came in view of the waiting crowds, they were cheered all the way to the banquet hall where Merlin stood waiting.

He pointed to the Round Table that filled the hall.

'Welcome, Arthur and Guinevere! Hail, our King and Queen! This Table seats a hundred and fifty knights; and each knight here will find his name carved upon a chair in letters of gold.'

At that the banquet commenced. Towards its close, Merlin rose again. After raising one last toast to King

Arthur and Queen Guinevere, he cleared his throat, then spoke in solemn tones.

'Today is the first day of the Knights of the Round Table; you all have your allotted chairs. And when one knight dies another will take his place, with the name on the seat changing by itself. Even so, the names of all knights who sit at this table will live forever. And in the years to come you will all have many strange and wonderful adventures.'

Merlin paused, then said, 'Alas, I shall not be here to witness them. I leave you now to the wise counsel of your king. I have taught him all the wisdom that I know. God bless you all.'

With that Merlin passed slowly through the hall and away into the night. No one saw him again, though a story had it that Nimue, the Lady of the Lake, guided him to a rocky cave beside the Lake at Avalon, and there he is sleeping until the Day of Judgement.

When Merlin had gone, King Arthur rose and called for silence.

'Noble knights,' he said, 'we must do without Merlin now, but we must never forget his teaching. Each of you must swear a sacred oath that you will be true and loyal knights. Never act unfairly. Never be unjust. And always show mercy to those who crave it. If you ever break those vows, you will forfeit your place at this table. Further, Knights of the Round Table, you must never do battle without just cause, nor fight for worldly goods.'

Each man stood and made his vow. And thereafter each repeated the vow every year at the Feast of Pentecost.

5

The Story of the Knight of the Garter

It was the first Christmastide following his wedding, and there was much merrymaking at King Arthur's court. Many noble knights were present, seated at the Round Table as true brothers, enjoying the feasting, singing, and happy talk.

The lovely green-eyed Queen Guinevere sat upon a dais beneath a canopy with silk curtains draped at her back. Rich tapestries from Toulouse and Turkestan hung around her, all embroidered with the costliest jewels. Beside her sat Arthur, proud and handsome, not eating until everyone was served, as was his custom.

Below the royal high table was the Round Table around which sat King Arthur's knights: each was served with twelve dishes, bright red wine, and good strong ale. The celebrations continued through the days and nights.

On New Year's Eve, when the merriment was at its height, the hall doors suddenly burst open and a rider came charging in. He was a giant of a man, surely the tallest man in the realm, with strong limbs and a great proud head. Yet despite his bulk he was fiercely handsome.

Great wonder spread throughout the hall at this odd sight. For the stranger was completely green from head to toe: both the clothing and the man himself. His coat and cloak were green with a lining of ermine fur; the hood upon his shoulders was green to match, as were his leather hose. He wore a green belt and well-fashioned green riding boots. And his mighty horse was of that same bright green, so that it matched the man exactly.

But most peculiar of all, the man was green himself: the long flowing hair that fell to his shoulders was as green as feather grass, as was the bushy beard that hung upon his chest. His face too was of a greenish hue. No one in the hall had ever seen so strange a sight.

Yet he wore no armour, carried no shield or lance. In one hand he held a holly branch—from the tree that is ever green when the leaves of others die—and in the other he held a huge axe, with a blade burnished bright and razor sharp.

Riding up to the royal dais, he wasted no words in greeting, shouting in a deep-throated roar, 'Where is the captain of this crew? I wish to have my say with him.'

He stared wildly about the hall, seeking out a man who would hold his gaze. But all present sat stony still in silence, awed by his brazen words.

At last Arthur rose and greeted the guest.

'Fellow, you are fair welcome. I am Arthur, head of this company. Leave your horse and join us, I pray you. You shall tell us later of yourself and your reasons for visiting my court.'

'It is not my wish to dally here,' the other said. 'I have

sought you out because your fame is known throughout Christendom; your court and company are counted as the best in courtesy and valour. You may be assured by the holly branch I bear that I come in peace and would part friends with you. Since I want no war I wear no metal plate; but should you be as bold as men believe, you will grant me a favour before I go.'

'Courteous knight,' said Arthur, 'if you crave a contest, then you shall surely have one.'

'No, fighting is far from my thoughts,' the knight replied. 'For I see nothing but beardless children in these pews; their might is puny beside mine. No, I called at your court to play a game since it is Yuletide when many young bloods seek sport. Is there anyone in this hall with enough red blood to strike one blow for another? I will give him my sharp axe and, if he be man enough to hold it, he may strike the first blow as hard as he desires. I shall not resist. However, within a twelve month, he shall receive the same from me. Well? Who dares accept my challenge?'

The green giant twisted round in the saddle, rolled his great green eyes, arched his bristling brows, and stroked his bushy beard, waiting for somebody to rise.

When no one moved he spoke again.

'Is this truly King Arthur's court whose fame is spoken of in every realm? See how the lords of the Round Table cower at the words of a defenceless man!'

And he laughed so loudly that Arthur's face grew red with shame, and he stepped towards the stranger, saying, 'Sir, now we see you are in earnest; if no one else will take up your challenge, give me your axe and I shall grant you the boon.'

Arthur advanced and took the weapon from him,

gripped the shaft and waited for the man to dismount. The green fellow stepped down and stood before Arthur, a full head taller than anyone at court. With a stern look he bent his head and calmly prepared to take the blow. 'Now, sir,' he said, 'before you take off my head, give me your word that you will fulfil our contract.'

'Whatever happens I shall take the blow,' said Arthur, 'twelve months hence by whatever weapon you choose. But tell me, what is your name and how am I to find you?'

The other smiled.

'I am well content that it is you who will strike the blow. Strike hard and cleanly, and you will straightaway hear of my name and house. Then follow in my footsteps at the appointed time. Now hold the axe steady and show us how it strikes.'

Thereupon, the green giant knelt upon the floor, bowed his head low and, brushing his long green hair forward over his face, he bared the nape of his neck ready for the blow.

Arthur gripped the axe and swung it high, his left foot set firmly forward; then he brought it down deftly upon the bare green neck. The sharp blade sliced through flesh and bone cleanly and cut it right in two, so that the axe head bit deep into the floor. The head was sent rolling back and forth among pairs of feet about the table. Blood gushed forth out of the body, bright red on green. Yet the fellow did not fall, he did not falter in the slightest. He stood up on stiff legs and, as everybody stared, he reached forward, picked up his head and held it aloft. Then, grasping the bridle of his green steed, he stepped up into the stirrup and mounted the horse, holding his head by the hair to face the king.

The severed head lifted its eyelids, stared with flashing eyes and opened its mouth wide so that all could hear the words, 'Arthur, do not forget our pact: seek hard until you find me, as you promised before these noble knights. Come to the Green Knight's Chapel at dawn on New Year's Day to receive just such a blow as you dealt me.'

With a sudden movement, he pulled his stallion round and rode swiftly from the hall, head in hand, sparks flying from the flashing hoofs. Nobody saw which way he went, just as no one had seen him come. Yet all who were witness to the scene swore it was a wonder beyond compare.

Arthur had the axe hung upon the wall so that men might stare in awe and tell the amazing tale.

The year went swiftly by. The cold cheer of Lent arrived, then the season of summer with its soft breezes, followed by Michaelmas when the moon hangs wintry pale in the night sky, until at last, on All Saints' Day, King Arthur held a feast before his quest.

After supper, Arthur took leave of his knights: the bold Sir Gawain and Sir Agravain-of-the-Heavy-Hand, Bishop Baldwin, and Yvain, son of Uriens, Sir Dodinal le Sauvage, Lionel, and Lucan the Good, Sir Bors, and Belvedere. Each gave him counsel, though in their hearts they feared he would not return. Last of all he kissed his dear wife, Guinevere—was this to be their last embrace?

'You all know the terms of my pact,' said Arthur to the company. 'I must entrust myself to God and take the stroke of that green man. Farewell.'

He rode through the realm with no one for company save his good mount Gringolet. On and on through many a long night he made his way to the northern coast of

Wales—remembering his boyhood encounters with the evil Vortigern as he spied the snow-capped peaks of Snowdonia. He continued past Holy Head, opposite the island of Anglesey; there he turned east across the Dee and made his way through the forest of Wirral.

Earnestly he enquired of each person he met: had they heard of a knight all in green or a Green Chapel thereabouts? But all said the same and solemnly swore they had never heard of such a knight.

Thus Arthur rode across the country until Christmas Eve when he found himself in a forest of huge oaks, their branches intertwined with bramble and hawthorn, so that he found it hard to make his way. Suddenly he was aware of a strange castle through the trees. He praised his luck that he had somewhere to spend Christmas Day. In answer to his call, a porter greeted him from the castle wall.

'Good sir, kindly enquire if your lord would permit a lodging here?'

The man soon returned with several servants. They let down the drawbridge, crossed over, and greeted the weary knight most politely. He was led across the bridge, helped down from his horse, and taken by a party of noble squires into a richly-furnished hall. A fire blazed fiercely upon the open hearth and Arthur warmed himself while awaiting the castle lord.

Soon the lord descended from his chamber to greet the guest.

'You are heartily welcome to my house,' he said. 'All you find here is at your disposal.'

'You are most kind, dear sir,' said Arthur.

Arthur looked at his host and thought how well suited he seemed to be master of such a mighty castle. He was tall and broad-shouldered, with a thick beaver-coloured beard, fiery red hair, and handsome face, proud and honest.

They passed into the parlour where the host had servants promptly attend to all King Arthur's needs: he was taken to a bower of the castle where the servants unbuckled his armour, washed and clothed him in rich flowing robes, then led him back to the hall and gave him a seat at the fire beside the castle lord. Attendants set a table down on trestles, covered it with a white cloth, and laid spoons of silver and a gold salt-cellar. They next brought in soups of every sort and sundry fish, some breaded, some broiled on coals, some simmered, some in stews steaming with spices and sauces. And all was washed down with refreshing wines.

'Tonight being Christmas Eve,' said the host, 'we fast on fish; tomorrow we shall see you sumptuously fed.'

Before the meal began, Lady Mary the host's wife, who had wished to see the king, came from her chamber accompanied by her maids. Her proud bearing and graceful manners were beyond praise.

She is almost as beautiful as Queen Guinevere herself, thought Arthur.

Upon her head she wore a tall head-dress hung with pearls, and her skin was as white and fair as the first snow fallen upon the hills. The lovely lady sat down beside King Arthur, ordering sweetmeats to be brought as refreshment and more wine to warm their hearts.

At the end of the evening Arthur was taken to his room and slept the night most soundly.

Three days were spent in feasting and Christmas celebrations, with singing and much good cheer. All the time the lady of the castle sat beside Arthur and attended to his every comfort. At last it was time to depart and Arthur took leave of the kind host. But the castle lord wished to know why he had strayed so far from his court at Christmastide.

'I seek the Green Chapel and the lone knight that lives there,' answered Arthur. 'We agreed to meet at this chapel on a certain day; and I have but three days to find it. I would rather die than fail in my errand.'

With a smile the lord said, 'But your search is over. Put your mind at rest. You may remain with me until the morn of New Year's Day, for the Green Chapel is but two miles from here. My groom will gladly show you the way.'

The host took his arm and seated him once more by the fireside.

'For three days,' he said, 'you shall stay here at your ease and sleep late since you will need all your strength for the coming trial. While you are resting I shall go hunting in the forest and my wife will entertain you.'

Bowing low, King Arthur gratefully gave his assent.

'Now, sire,' said the host, 'let us strike a bargain: whatever I gain in the forest I will give you on my return, and you will give me all that you have earned in my castle.'

'That sounds a fair bargain to me,' laughed Arthur, 'for I am sure I stand to gain most by it!'

At dawn next day, master and servants rode off across the frosty ground following the keen-nosed hounds. And while the good lord led the hunt for deer in a linden wood, Arthur lay in bed, lingering long after the pale sun had risen. As he lay beneath his warm coverlet in the curtained bed, he suddenly caught the sound of a door opening softly. Pulling back one corner of the curtain he was surprised to see the lord's lovely wife enter and approach his bed. So surprised was Arthur that he laid his head low again, pretending to be asleep.

Lady Mary stole towards him, pulled aside the curtain and sat down softly on the bed, waiting for him to awake. For a long while he feigned sleep, wondering what to do: it ill became an honourable knight to betray his host's trust. At last, he stirred and stretched, as if startled from sleep; he opened his eyes wide in wonder at the lady's presence.

She spoke sweetly, gazing fondly at him, her laughing lips inviting.

'Good morning, King Arthur, you are a heavy sleeper to let a maiden slip in unnoticed. Since I have caught you unawares, you must grant me a favour.'

'Good morrow, dear lady,' said Arthur brightly. 'Ask what you will of me, I surrender myself to your good graces. And if you will permit your prisoner to rise, I shall swiftly put on something more befitting a lady's presence.'

'Not so, sweet sir,' said the smiling lady. 'You shall not rise from your bed; I wish to keep you captive for a while. All the world knows of your courtesy to ladies and I wish to test it for myself. You see, we are alone here; my lord and his men are long departed. The door is locked and since I have you in my power I could satisfy my own desire and yours as well.'

'In faith,' said Arthur, 'what a wonderful prize you offer; no man could refuse it. Alas, however, I am unworthy of your praise: would that my deeds could ever aspire to the prize you promise.'

Lady Mary continued to flatter him with the sweetest words. But the king resisted.

'You are bound to a better man,' he told her. 'Yet I

am greatly honoured by the kindness you offer me and I shall ever be your humble servant.'

Thus they talked until nearly noon, Lady Mary conversing in words of love, the noble knight framing his defence.

At last she rose to leave, saying sadly, 'You are not the man I know by reputation. He would never have lain by a maiden's side without claiming at least one kiss in courtesy.'

'Good lady,' said Arthur, 'I grant a kiss most gladly.'

With that she took him in her arms, bent down her head and kissed him full upon the lips, then departed in silence.

Arthur did not linger in bed a moment longer; he was up, dressed, and away to mass as quickly as he could, and he spent the rest of the day in company until the cold moon rose. It was then that the lord returned.

'What think you, sir, of this?' he cried joyfully on seeing Arthur, showing him the many hinds and does he had killed that day.

'In truth,' said Arthur, 'the game is the finest I have seen at this season of the year.'

'I give it to you, sire,' said the kindly host, 'according to our pact.'

'That being so,' said the king, 'I shall repay you what I earned today within these castle walls.'

Thereupon he embraced the host and kissed him heartily.

'Such a gift,' said the lord, 'I gladly accept. But tell me, where did you earn such a fine reward? I am anxious to learn the source.'

'That was not part of our agreement,' said Arthur. 'Press me no further; you have had all that we agreed.'

With jokes and laughter they conversed, ate a hearty supper of roast venison washed down with the best red wines and, at close of day, agreed to fulfil on the morrow the same pact as on the day before: that the two should trade whatever each won that day. Then finally they said goodnight, for the hour was late.

Before the barnyard cock had crowed, the lord was out of bed and away deep into the woods. Meanwhile, the king slept on beneath his silken canopy. Just as the day was dawning, however, Lady Mary crept into the room and sat down beside his bed. This time he thought it best to greet her right away and she repaid him with soft words, settling closely at his side.

'Sir, if you really are King Arthur,' she sighed, 'it seems great wonder that you have learned nothing from yesterday's lesson, though I painted it as plain as my poor wits allowed.'

'What lesson, dear lady?' he asked alarmed. 'Pray, forgive me if I have failed you.'

'My lesson in kissing,' came the answer. 'Where he has found favour, it becomes a knight to claim freely what is his.'

'Dismiss such thoughts, dear lady,' he said. 'Such liberties, I fear, would deeply offend you.'

'I would not resist,' she said.

'I could not insult you by taking what is not mine to claim,' he replied. 'But I would not deny you a gift that is freely granted: you may kiss me again if you wish.'

Lady Mary kissed him twice upon the lips, and the two talked as friends. As soon as she had gone, he rose and made ready for mass, spent the day talking with the household, and awaiting the lord's return.

When at dusk the huntsmen returned, the master

41

greeted Arthur cheerily and showed him the wild boar he'd caught.

'Now, sir,' he said, 'the boar is yours by our agreement.'

'I thank you,' said King Arthur, 'and I give you all that I gained here while you were gone.' Thereupon he clasped the host about the neck and kissed him heartily upon both cheeks.

'By Saint Giles,' the host replied, 'you are the luckiest man I've ever met.'

That night at supper the host's fair lady treated Arthur to stolen glances that stirred his heart. But he could not in conscience repay her courtship, though he took all pains to please her. At the end of supper, the host proposed that they renew their pact for New Year's Eve, but Arthur asked to be excused, saying he had to leave at dawn to pursue his quest.

The host protested, 'I give you my word that by dawn on New Year's Day you shall be at the Green Chapel. I cannot permit you to leave just yet. Stay and lie in your warm bed while I am hunting. Hold to our terms and trade your winnings with me; I have tested you twice and found you true, tomorrow the third payment will be due.'

Arthur finally agreed, so they drank a last draught of wine and went to bed.

Early next day, the lord rode off into the clear, crisp morning in search of game. In the meantime, the king lay in wholesome sleep. But since love would permit her no repose, Lady Mary was awake at dawn. Following her heart, she went to Arthur's chamber and, lying at his side, greeted him with a kiss while he, chivalrous as ever, welcomed her politely.

As the king gazed upon her, so faultless of feature, so beautiful, his heart surged within him. But, with gentle laughter, he lightly turned aside her tender advances. Finally, she said with a heartfelt sigh, 'How can you be so cold towards me?'

'Dear lady,' said Arthur, 'I love only my lady Guinevere, and I shall always be true to her. I mean you no offence, but I have already pledged my love.'

'Then let me kiss you three times in parting,' she said sadly, 'and I shall leave you, lamenting as a maiden spurned.'

As he inclined his head, she kissed him lovingly, then sighing said, 'Before we part, pray let me give you a token of my love.'

And she handed him a ruby ring that flashed before his eyes like the fiery sun. But he dismissed it.

'Before God, dear lady, I forego all gifts. I have none to offer and will take none in return.'

'If you refuse my ring,' she persisted, 'I shall give you my silk garter to keep you from harm in your trials to come.'

Thereupon she removed a green silk garter from her thigh, pressing it upon him and pleading that he take it. He dearly wished to refuse but, thinking it might bring good luck in his ordeal, he finally accepted.

When Lady Mary had gone, the king jumped out of bed and dressed, putting the green garter beneath his coat. No sooner had the lord returned than Arthur set to kissing him three times as earnestly as he could.

'By heaven,' said the host, 'you have had some luck since you took up this kissing game. Is there anything else you gained?'

'I think not,' the king replied at once, blushing. He

had not given his host the hidden garter—fearing to betray his wife.

'Now,' said the other, 'my gift is poor: I hunted all day and have nothing save this foul-smelling fox brush. Poor payment for three kisses!'

With much laughter, they dined together, drank and made merry as such good men might until it was getting late. Then off to their beds they went content.

The night passed, New Year's Day drew on, daylight dispelled the gloom, and grey clouds cast down their snow. Though he kept his eyes closed, King Arthur slept little, counting each crow of the cock and listening long to the wind wailing through the yews. Before dawn he rose and dressed himself in armour, putting his love-gift, the lady's garter, round his thigh.

While the household slept, he made his way into the courtyard. He found his good steed Gringolet waiting with a groom eager to show the way. Arthur mounted his horse, struck its sides with his spurs, and rode out of the castle across the drawbridge.

They rode through a forest of bare boughs with steep banks rising on either side. Then they climbed high hills covered in frozen snow and galloped over mist-mantled moors until, just as the sun was rising, they reached a lofty hilltop above a valley.

'You are close by the Green Chapel now,' said the groom. 'Take the narrow track down yonder slope until you reach the valley, then bear left and you will soon see it. Farewell, Your Majesty, God be with you.'

Arthur picked his way down the track and soon found himself riding across a wild, god-forsaken valley. Not a soul or dwelling was to be seen except, in the distance, what seemed like a grass-covered hillock hard by a flowing stream. Riding up to it and dismounting, he found the green mound was hollow like a cave.

'Can this be the Green Chapel?' he wondered.

Visor down and lance in hand, he advanced towards the cave. All of a sudden, he heard his name called from behind a crag on the distant bank.

'Arthur, halt now and receive your due.'

Round the crag appeared the Green Knight, bearing an axe with a curved broad blade. When they were standing face to face, the green giant said, 'Ah, my friend, it seems your word holds good. You have followed me faithfully to settle the business on which we both agreed. A year ago you struck me a blow; now you must give me a chance to do the same. Take off your helmet, bow down your head, and do not flinch.'

'I shall not flinch,' said Arthur. 'Strike away, I have no fear.'

With that he knelt down and fearlessly bared his neck before the blade. The green man gathered his strength, heaved the heavy axe above his head and, grim-faced, prepared to deal a massive blow. Arthur, meanwhile, glanced up just as the axe descended and his shoulders quivered just a mite.

At once, the huge man stayed his blow, saying scornfully, 'Do you call yourself brave? I did not quake when you struck me; yet you quiver at the mere swishing of my axe. What a coward you are!'

'Strike again,' said Arthur. 'I shall not flinch this time. Go on, man, get it over with, for God's sake.'

'Have at you then,' the other cried.

And heaving the axe aloft, the Green Knight brought it down with a blood-curdling scream. Yet once again he stayed his hand before drawing blood. This time, however,

Arthur remained as firm as an oak, neither glancing up, nor flinching. 'Now you have recovered your nerve,' the Green Knight said, 'I may strike truly at King Arthur's nape. Keep your neckbone clear, I shall now deliver the final blow.'

Arthur said grimly, 'I tire of your threats. Finish the job if you are man enough.'

With that the green man brought the axe down on the king's neck. Yet the blow merely parted the skin, freeing a trickle of red blood.

When Arthur felt the wound and saw his blood upon the snow, he sprang up, drew his sword and shouted, 'I have borne the blow, as we agreed; if you strike again I will defend myself, for you are repaid.'

The green giant lowered his axe.

'Bold fellow,' he said gently, 'put out your fire. I owed you a blow and you have borne it. The first blow and the second were for promises truly kept—for the kisses that my wife gave you. And each you restored to me. But you failed at the third attempt and therefore earned the cut. For that is my sash about your thigh. I know well the number of kisses and your noble conduct too—it was my scheme to test you. I hold you to be the most faultless man to walk this earth. Yet you were disloyal in concealing the garter. I forgive you that, since it was done in respect for my wife.'

'I am ashamed, sir,' said Arthur, handing him the green garter. 'Pray, take this symbol of my shame.'

The other laughed. 'You have borne my blade and are forgiven. Keep the garter so that you might be ever mindful of our pact. Now, return with me and make your peace with my wife; we shall complete our feasting in good cheer.'

But Arthur declined.

'I have lingered long enough,' he said. 'Please commend me to Lady Mary; I must now return to court. However, I gladly take the silk garter: it will remind me always of the weakness of the flesh.'

The two men embraced and parted. In due course, Arthur arrived safely back at Camelot and everyone was overjoyed to see him. Solemnly he told what had passed at the Green Knight's Chapel.

The knights decided that all the lords and ladies belonging to King Arthur's court would wear a band of green for Arthur's sake. It would be a token of their fellowship. And when a knight distinguished himself in chivalry, he was made Knight of the Garter—the highest order of the realm.

Upon the band of green they had inscribed the words: HONY SOYT QUI MAL Y PENSE (Shame on him who evil thinks).

6

The Revenge of Morgana Le Fay

When Uther Pendragon, Arthur's father, had fallen in love with Igraine, she was already married—to Gorlois, Duke of Cornwall. But Uther killed Gorlois in a duel. For this cruel act, Igraine's daughter Morgana Le Fay never forgave Uther; and when he died, she held Arthur responsible for his father's sins.

One day, she vowed, she would have her revenge. And all through the time when Arthur was growing up, Morgana studied the black arts and sorcery. Now her time was drawing near.

In a tumbledown stone chapel deep in the forest, the dark-eyed, black-haired, black-hearted Morgana was surrounded by books of magic and her crystal ball. She was forever brewing mischief in her great cauldron, filling it with magical ingredients for her spells: frogs' toes, bats' wings, cuckoo spit, juniper juice, and suchlike.

At last she got the mixture right. Rubbing her hands with glee, she gave a cruel laugh.

'Now I can have my revenge and put an end to Arthur!'

Her plan was fiendish and cunning.

One day, soon after his return from the Green Chapel, Arthur was hunting in the company of his knights. And it so happened that he and Sir Accolon of Gaul lost the others as they chased a mighty stag. So far did they ride, over hills and bogs, mile after mile, that eventually their horses fell dead beneath them, and they had to continue on foot.

But the stag grew weary too, and soon it had to stop to drink at a dark lake in the middle of the forest. It was there, at the lakeside, that Arthur drew his sword and ran it through.

As the two knights stood over their prize, they were surprised to see a small ship, all hung with silken sails, gliding towards them over the still waters of the lake. On and on it came until its prow ground into the sands where they were standing; it seemed to invite them on board. Yet not a soul was to be seen.

'Come, sir,' said King Arthur to his companion, 'let us go and unravel the mystery of this ship.'

So the two men stepped aboard and found the ship carpeted and curtained with the costliest silks and cloths, furnished with finely-carved chairs and tables. Dark night descended as they searched the hold; and when they emerged on deck they found a hundred torches blazing all along the sides—so that it was as light as day. Although the ship had seemed deserted, twelve young maidens suddenly appeared to welcome King Arthur and Sir Accolon, curtsying to the king.

'We bid you welcome, King Arthur,' they said in chorus. 'We are here to refresh you.'

With that they led the knights into a room where a white-clothed table was set with the most inviting meats and wines. The two men marvelled at the sumptuous spread; they had never seen a better meal.

When they had eaten and drunk all they desired, they were taken to separate cabins: each was richly furnished and had a bed enclosed by silken drapes. Since both men were weary from the hunt and lulled by the heady wine, they were soon sleeping soundly in their beds, and they slumbered on throughout the night.

It was late morning when King Arthur awoke: to his dismay, gone were the cosy bed and rich cabin; instead he found himself lying on the cold stone floor of a castle dungeon. But he was not alone. Through the darkness came groans and laments of other captives.

'Who are you?' called Arthur. 'Why do you complain?'

In the lull that followed, a tormented voice replied, 'We are twenty knights held prisoner here. Some of us have languished in this dungeon for nigh on seven years.'

'What is your crime?' Arthur asked.

'The lord of this castle, Sir Damas, is the most evil knight alive, and the greatest coward in the realm. He has a younger brother, Sir Onslake, a noble knight well loved by all; but Sir Damas refuses him his inheritance. So Sir Onslake sent us, his best knights, as emissaries to his brother; but the traitor seized and bound us once we were inside the castle, and threw us into this dungeon. Many a good knight has already starved to death. And we too will surely die, for we are too weak to stand.'

'God save us all,' said Arthur.

As they were talking, a maiden came into the dungeon, asking Arthur how he was.

'I cannot say, fair lady,' he replied. 'For I know not why I am here or what is to be my fate.'

'Then I will tell you,' she said sweetly. 'You have been chosen by my lord to fight on his behalf. He has nominated you his champion in a joust. If you agree, your life will be spared; if you refuse, you will stay here till the end of your days.'

'I would rather fight and die than rot in prison,' said Arthur. 'But I will only fight if these knights are freed as well.'

'So be it,' she said after a pause.

'Then prepare a horse and armour,' he said.

As his eyes grew accustomed to the gloom, Arthur stared hard into her face.

'Dear lady, surely I have seen you at Camelot?' he said.

'No, no, no,' she said hastily. 'I am the daughter of Sir Damas and have lived here all my life.'

But she was lying. For she was lady-in-waiting to Morgana Le Fay.

Meanwhile, several miles away, Sir Accolon of Gaul was also awaking from a deep sleep; and he was alarmed to find himself lying not in his warm bed, but on the edge of a deep well. He only had to move a fraction and he would plunge to the bottom of the well.

Swiftly rolling to safety, he stared about him, wondering how he had come to be in that strange courtyard. There could be no doubt: he and King Arthur had been enchanted by the maidens on the ship.

'Those creatures were demons not women,' he muttered.

'If I escape this adventure unharmed, I will slay all women who use charms and spells.'

Just at that moment, a strange dwarf appeared—an ugly fellow with a large crooked mouth and a spade-like nose.

Bowing low to Sir Accolon, he announced in a rasping voice, 'I come from Dame Morgana Le Fay; she sends you her fondest greetings and begs you be of good cheer. She thinks of you constantly and has a mission for you: she wishes you to be her champion . . . tomorrow at noon. You are to fight a knight who has offended her honour. Here, I bring you Excalibur, King Arthur's sword, so that no harm shall come to you. If you love my lady, you will bring her the knight's head; then she will marry you and make you her king.'

'I would willingly defend my lady's honour,' sighed Sir Accolon to himself. 'And since this fellow brings Excalibur, there can be no doubt he is from Morgana herself. All those enchantments must be her doing, so that I might do battle with her enemy.'

He embraced the dwarf, saying aloud, 'Convey my greetings to your mistress and tell her I will gladly be her champion—or die in the attempt.'

The dwarf then vanished as suddenly as he had come. Not long after, a knight rode by accompanied by six squires: it was Sir Onslake, noble brother of the evil Sir Damas. He greeted Sir Accolon and asked him his business.

'I am here to fight in just cause at noon tomorrow,' the bold knight replied.

Sir Onslake was overjoyed, thinking that this knight was to be his champion against his brother's knight. For a messenger from his brother had come that day to challenge his best knight to a joust to decide their differences. Sir Damas's champion would fight Sir Onslake's champion to the death.

But since Sir Onslake's best knights had been slain or taken prisoner by his wicked brother, he had no one to represent his cause. And now the brave Sir Accolon had volunteered—or so he thought.

'Come home with me and rest, dear sir,' Sir Onslake said. 'You shall dine with me and my lady wife; my servants will bathe and dress you, and prepare the best horse in my stable.'

So Sir Accolon followed the lord through the courtyard into the manor hall where attendants were waiting to wash and dress him in fine linen. When he had eaten well with the master and mistress, he was led to a chamber where he spent a restful night. Next morning he was clad in armour, with a helmet on his head; then he was seated on a white warhorse and led by a squire to a green meadow, not far from Sir Damas's castle.

Meanwhile, that same morning after mass, King Arthur was similarly attired in armour with a helmet on his head, and then seated on a black charger ready for battle. A squire led him likewise to the meadow where a great crowd had gathered to watch the joust.

Both knights were attended by six squires and rode their mounts behind the respective lords: Sir Damas and Sir Onslake.

As Arthur waited on his horse, he suddenly heard a woman's voice calling to him, 'Sire, I come from your dear sister, Morgana Le Fay; she sends you your sword Excalibur, for she has learned of the mortal danger you are in. Here is the sword in its scabbard; my mistress prays for your success. God be with you.'

Arthur felt the sword placed in his hand and the scabbard tied to his waist; and he thanked the maiden warmly. Now he knew he could not fail to win.

Both knights sat impatiently on their steeds at either end of the field, their visors down, waiting for the joust to start. Neither knew who his opponent was. At the given signal—a trumpet blast—the two men charged full tilt at one another, lances at the ready. They struck each other's shield so fiercely that both men and mounts crashed to the ground.

The two knights rose together, swords raised high, and struck at each other wildly, as powerfully as they could. Yet always King Arthur's sword failed to pierce his enemies guard as the other's did his: with every stroke he delivered, Accolon drew blood; yet he bore hardly a scratch from Arthur's blows.

Soon Arthur was so badly wounded that it was a marvel he stood his ground. Accolon now advanced, sword drawn, to finish off his foe. He brought down the weapon with all his might—but the blow just split Arthur's helmet as he rolled aside. Pulling himself up, the wounded Arthur, blood streaming down his face and blocking his eyes, got in an answering thrust that well nigh felled Sir Accolon.

They fought fiercely together until their breath failed. Then, having rested, they both came at each other once again, panting hard and groaning with the pain; they cut and thrust until the muddy soil ran red with blood. By this time Arthur had seven gaping wounds that gushed forth blood, any one of which would have caused the death of a normal man.

All who witnessed the duel paled at the sight of such bloody carnage. The two knights' coats of mail were torn to shreds and their bodies were now unprotected from blows on every side.

Arthur, maddened by the way he had been deceived— for he now saw that Excalibur was in his rival's hands— made one last despairing lunge; he brought his sword down so fiercely that it broke in two.

Sir Accolon laughed at his helpless victim, and advanced to deal the fatal blow. There was surely no escape.

'Sir Knight,' cried Accolon, 'you are beaten; you are swordless and have lost much blood. I do not wish to kill you, so yield to me.'

'No,' said Arthur firmly through clenched teeth. 'I would rather die a hundred deaths than yield to any man; though I lack a sword, I do not lack honour. I will not shame my knightly vows.'

'Well,' said Accolon, 'I do not share your shame. Have at you! Prepare to receive the fatal blow.'

Thereupon Accolon, his sword held high above Arthur's head, brought it down as hard as he could. But Arthur took the blow on his shield and struck back with his sword hilt, sending Accolon staggering three paces back. That was Arthur's chance.

As Accolon fell back, Excalibur twisted from his grasp and landed on the ground at Arthur's feet. As soon as the king grabbed its hilt he knew at once it was his sword.

'You have been too long from me, Excalibur,' he said, 'and much damage you have done.'

With that, before Accolon could recover, Arthur sprang forward, seized the scabbard from his belt and tossed it to one side.

'Now, Sir Knight,' said Arthur, 'you have spilt much

red blood with this sword today; now it is your blood that will run.'

And he leapt at Accolon, knocking him to the ground so hard that blood burst from his mouth, nose, and ears. Standing over the stricken knight, King Arthur cried, 'Yield or you will die!'

'Go ahead and slay me,' gasped Accolon, coughing blood. 'I too am bound by knightly vows and will never yield. I would rather die than live in shame. But I'll tell you this before I die: you are the best knight I've ever fought, and it is no shame to die by your hand.'

As Accolon was speaking, Arthur thought he recognized his voice.

'You are a brave man, Sir Knight,' said Arthur, lowering his sword. 'But tell me: where are you from and what is your name?'

'I am from King Arthur's court,' said Accolon; 'my name is Sir Accolon of Gaul.' It was like a knife in Arthur's heart.

He suddenly saw it all: the spell put on them aboard the ship, the twelve enchantresses, the dungeon and the brothers' feud, the false sword from his sister . . . Of course, it had all been arranged by Morgana Le Fay to have him killed.

'Tell me,' he murmured sadly, 'who gave you this sword?'

'Why, Dame Morgana Le Fay,' replied Sir Accolon.

And he told Arthur the story of the dwarf, his love for Morgana, his vow to be her champion, and her promise to marry him once he had delivered his opponent's head.

'This accursed sword has brought my death,' said Accolon finally. 'But who are you that Morgana wants dead so badly?'

'Oh, Accolon,' said Arthur, 'do you not know me? I am your king.'

When Accolon heard that, he cried out, 'Oh, my God, have mercy on me. Forgive me, sire, I did not know you.'

'God forgives you,' said Arthur, 'for the battle was not your doing. It was my sister, Morgana Le Fay, who used magic to get you to agree. She deceived us both, and she will be made to pay, I swear.'

All the knights and ladies who had witnessed the battle wept for pity. Then Arthur called Sir Damas and Sir Onslake together.

To Sir Damas he said, 'You, sir, are not worthy of your knightly vows. You are a coward and a villain. Therefore, I command that you give your brother your castle and all its household; all you shall have is a horse on which to ride away from these lands. And I charge you, on pain of death, to compensate the twenty knights you kept prisoner.'

To Sir Onslake, King Arthur said, 'Because you are a good knight, true and gentle in all your deeds, I invite you to my court. But first tell me where I and Sir Accolon may rest and have our wounds tended.'

'Sire,' said Sir Onslake, 'I will take you both to an abbey. The nuns will dress your wounds and care for you until you are well.'

When they arrived at the abbey, the nuns cleaned and dressed their wounds as best they could. But Accolon was too far gone: he had lost so much blood he died within days. Arthur regained his health and was soon able to leave the abbey. Before he left, he ordered that Sir Accolon's body be placed upon a bier.

'Bear the body to my sister, Morgana Le Fay,' he said

grimly. 'Tell her it is my gift to her. Inform her, too, that I now have Excalibur, and she will soon feel its steel!'

Arthur left the abbey and rode to Camelot where Queen Guinevere and his knights were overjoyed to see him. And when they heard of his strange adventures, the death of the bold Sir Accolon and the evil of Morgana Le Fay, they all called for Morgana to be burnt at the stake.

However, as they were having supper in the great hall that night, a young woman arrived, bearing a finely-embroidered cloak; it glittered with pearls and rubies and was trimmed with sable and ermine.

To King Arthur, the woman humbly said, 'My lord, I come from your sister, Morgana Le Fay; she begs forgiveness. The devil that possessed her has now gone; she acted in a madness caused by grief. In penitence she now sends you this gift. When you wear this cloak, you will never again suffer pain.'

King Arthur was moved by the woman's words, and held out his hand to take the cloak. But just at that moment, Nimue, the Lady of the Lake, suddenly appeared.

'Wait, sire,' she said, hand on his arm. 'I must speak with you.'

She whispered in his ear, so that no one else could hear: 'Do not put on this cloak. Let Morgana's envoy try it first.'

Turning to the bearer of the cloak, Arthur said, 'I thank you for your gift, but I wish to see it on you first.'

A look of terror showed in the woman's eyes.

'Oh, no, sire. I am not worthy of such a royal robe.'

Arthur shouted angrily, 'But you *will* wear it before it touches my own back!'

Motioning to two knights to hold her still, the king

took the cloak and put it over the woman's shoulders as she squirmed and screamed.

Then he and his knights witnessed a terrible sight.

The cloak and the woman burst into sudden, all-consuming flames. Within seconds all that was left was a pile of grey ash upon the floor.

When she heard the news, Morgana fled across the sea to Gaul to escape King Arthur's wrath. Before his court, King Arthur vowed, 'One day I shall take revenge on my sister. Mark my words well.'

7

Arthur Betrayed

S ome time after his escape from the sorcery of Morgana Le Fay, King Arthur was hunting in the forest near Camelot. He had not gone far when he came upon a wounded knight, groaning in great pain. And well he might: for a sword was buried in his chest, pinning him to the ground. Clearly, there was little the king could do.

'Tell me, good knight,' said Arthur, kneeling beside the stricken man, 'shall I bring you a priest or leeches to ease the pain?'

King Arthur was surprised at the man's reply.

'Neither, sire. I wish to be carried to King Arthur's court where I may be healed. Nimue, Lady of the Lake, has foretold that I will be cured by the best knight of all— he has only to lay his hand on me and withdraw the sword, and I shall be fit and well.'

Arthur was puzzled. Who was this best knight at his court? How could he heal a dying man?

'Well, tomorrow is the Feast of Pentecost,' said the

king. 'All the knights of the Round Table will be at Camelot to renew their vows. I'll have you brought to court and we will see if anyone can help.'

So Arthur had the wounded man carried on a litter to Camelot, made as comfortable as his wound allowed, then placed upon the floor, close to the fire for warmth. Meanwhile, the knights took their allotted seats around the table, and each in turn stood up to relate acts of chivalry in the year just passed; then each renewed his vow of knighthood.

When the ceremony was over, King Arthur commanded the knights to lay a hand upon the wounded man. Each touched the knight and prayed fervently for his soul. Yet he groaned as loudly as before.

All at once, a trumpet call rang out, and into the hall strode a young squire dressed in white, led by the Lady of the Lake herself. The fellow was fair-haired and broad-shouldered, with just the wisp of a beard upon his chin; he was so tall and handsome that the ladies present blushed, while all colour drained from Queen Guinevere's face. As their eyes met the young squire faltered in his stride, his heart pierced so deeply that there and then he vowed to serve none other but the queen.

The Lady Nimue's voice cut through the wondering silence of the court.

'My lord King Arthur, I come to fulfil Merlin's last request; for before he left this mortal life, he instructed this youth to come here at Pentecost to claim his place at your table. Sire, I bring you Lancelot, son of King Pant and Queen Elaine of Gwynedd; ever since his parents were slain by the evil King Ryon, he has been under my protection—thus he will be known henceforth as Sir Lancelot of the Lake. I commend him to you as the best knight in Christendom.'

Even as she was speaking, all faces turned to an empty seat at the table as the name LANCELOT appeared in letters of gold.

King Arthur rose, drew his sword Excalibur and laid it upon both shoulders of the squire, dubbing him knight.

'Arise, Sir Lancelot of the Lake,' he said with a smile. 'Welcome into the noble company of knights. Come, take your rightful place.'

Now, all the while, the sorely-wounded knight had been groaning on his litter; hope flickered in his bloodshot eyes as he followed the knighting of Lancelot. And when Arthur had returned to his seat, Nimue led Sir Lancelot over to the wounded man. Without a word, the newly-made knight bent down, placed one hand on the man's brow and, with the other, gently drew out the bloodstained sword.

To everyone's astonishment, the gaping wound closed up instantly, the pain on the knight's face eased and he stood up completely healed.

Thereupon, Nimue curtsied low to King Arthur, kissed Sir Lancelot tenderly on the cheek, and turned to go. Yet, before she left the hall, she spoke these words:

'That is Sir Lancelot's first deed of knighthood. The second time he heals a man, however, will be his last; and it will mark the beginning of the end of this noble fellowship.'

With that she was gone.

King Arthur did not dwell long on the fateful words. So pleased was he to welcome the handsome young knight that he gave it no further thought.

But not all those at the table rejoiced at the knighting of an untried squire; after all, he had performed no test of strength, no valiant deeds. There was one knight present who muttered into his beard against the callow youth: that was Sir Mordred, son of Morgana Le Fay. One day he was to reveal Lancelot's dark secret and betray him to the king—but that was in the future; for the moment, he kept his tongue behind his teeth.

In the years to come, Lancelot stilled the wagging tongues: for he soon gained the greatest reputation of any knight in the whole of Christendom. No one could match him in strength and skill, in chivalrous deed and noble thought and the king and queen both loved him dearly. Yet that love was to be their undoing: for while Arthur's was that of a father to a son, Guinevere's grew into a love more fond and dangerous.

From his first day at court, Lancelot had loved Queen Guinevere, and all his deeds of valour were dedicated to her. Arthur felt no jealousy, for he never doubted the loyalty of Lancelot or his queen; he was proud that Lancelot should be her champion and wear her colours. Nor was there the slightest cause to doubt. No one, however, saw the lengthening shadow of destiny creeping into their lives, or the threads being woven into a tangled web that one day would entrap them all.

It all began quite innocently in the merry month of May when, as all true lovers know, every flower and tree, just like every loving heart, begins to blossom and sing.

While King Arthur, Sir Lancelot, and other knights were hunting in the forest about Camelot, Queen Guinevere called together her trusty knights—those young men whose duty it was to guard and serve the queen. There were among them King Arthur's boyhood friend Sir Kay, Sir Ironside, Knight of the Red Lands, Sir Dodinas le Sauvage,

Sir Pelleas, Sir Ozanna le Cure Hardy, and Sir Ladinas of the Wild Forest.

When they had all gathered, the queen said, 'In the month of May, men's and women's hearts should fill with love. So I command you to dress in green and prepare your mounts; for we are to go riding in the greenwood. I shall bring ten ladies so that each knight shall accompany a lady, and each lady a knight.'

They formed a riding party and rode out through the trees.

In the meantime, King Arthur and his knights had come upon a foreign knight led by Nimue. His name was Sir Urry and he was being borne by his squires to King Arthur's court to seek a cure for his wounds. He had been on pilgrimages to all the courts of Europe for help; but none was found. Now he had come to Britain to seek King Arthur's aid.

'Sire,' said Nimue to Arthur, 'this poor knight may be healed only by the best knight at your court.'

Arthur at once summoned Sir Lancelot to attend to the man: as the knight knelt down and laid his hands on Sir Urry's head, the pain instantly departed and he was as fit as he had been before his wound.

All the knights cheered and shouted, clapping Sir Lancelot on the back.

'You are truly the best knight in Christendom,' cried King Arthur.

While King Arthur's party resumed their hunting, many miles distant the woods rang with happy shouts and laughter from Guinevere's band. They did not know that danger lurked in the dark thickets ahead.

By unhappy chance, the party was spotted by a knight named Meliagaunt, son of King Bagdemagus; he had his castle just seven miles from Camelot. For some time the knight had nurtured a secret love for the queen and, when he spotted her riding with just a handful of unarmed men, he saw that his chance had come. So he laid an ambush, surrounding the party with a hundred archers and twenty men-at-arms. Unsuspecting, the queen, her knights and ladies rode into the trap.

Sir Meliagaunt strode forward, sword in hand, and seized the bridle of Guinevere's horse.

'I declare my love for you, madam,' he said. 'I have been patient, but now I claim my prize.'

'What a traitor you are,' the queen cried in fury. 'Have you no shame? Would you dishonour the noble king who made you a knight? I would slit my own throat before I submitted to you!'

'Nothing you say will change my mind,' cried Sir Meliagaunt.

As they were speaking, the ten loyal knights had formed a ring around the queen and her ladies; and now Sir Kay stepped forward, declaring boldly, 'We will not allow you to shame our queen; even though we have no arms, we will not surrender to you.'

There was nothing for it but to fight. It was an uneven struggle, though the knights fought as bravely as they could. As Sir Meliagaunt's men bore down on them with lances and swords, the valiant ten wrestled weapons from their hands and used them to drive the enemy back. After a while, however, six brave knights lay bleeding on the ground, cut down by flying arrows and sword blows; the remaining four fought on stubbornly until their strength and blood gave out, though not before they had slain forty of the foe.

When the queen saw that her knights would soon be

slain, she cried out, 'Enough! Spare my men and I will go with you. If you kill them, you had better kill me too— for you will not take me alive!'

The traitor knight, Sir Meliagaunt, then called off the assault and had the wounded put on horseback. As swiftly as he could, he had them all taken with the queen to his castle, for he feared that news of his treachery would soon reach King Arthur.

As the procession made its way to the castle, the queen, unnoticed, called a young lad to her; he was less badly wounded than the rest and she charged him as follows, 'When you get an opportunity, ride like the wind and inform the king.'

So the lad bided his time, then suddenly dug his spurs hard into his horse's flanks, galloping away at full speed. Although Sir Meliagaunt's men gave chase and fired a hail of arrows after him, he got safely away and reached Camelot just as King Arthur was returning from the hunt.

When they heard the story, King Arthur and his knights were furious, thirsting for revenge. Sir Lancelot was the first to act.

'Sire, let me go on ahead; I'll reach the traitor quicker on my own. Follow as soon as you have gathered a well-armed band of men.'

Arthur readily agreed—there was no time to lose; and Lancelot raced off as fast as his steed would go, flying like an arrow to the traitor's den. He forded rivers, swam with his horse through swirling streams, and soon came to the clearing where the ten bold knights had fought—he recognized it from the broken trees and blood-soaked soil. Then he followed the bloodied trail until he came to a wood; and there before him stood a line of thirty archers, their arrows pointing at his heart.

'Halt! You shall not pass!' their leader cried.

But the gallant knight charged straight at them, not heeding their arrows, until he was running with blood and his horse fell dead, pierced by a dozen shafts. Lancelot took cover in ditch and bush, avoiding the waiting men; after making a wide detour, he rejoined the track behind Sir Meliagaunt's knights.

He had not gone far on foot when he came upon two men driving a cartful of logs. 'Carter,' he said to one of the men, 'permit me to ride with you the two miles to the castle.'

'I am fetching wood for my lord Sir Meliagaunt,' said the man roughly; 'I do not aid his enemies.'

At that Sir Lancelot struck the man so hard he fell senseless to the ground, and his companion shouted out, 'Fair knight, spare my life and I'll take you anywhere you want.'

So the second carter drove him at a gallop towards the castle; within half an hour, they were passing through the gates. At that moment, one of Queen Guinevere's ladies happened to glance through a window; and she cried out to the queen, 'Look, madam, an armed knight comes riding in a woodman's cart.'

As Queen Guinevere looked out she recognized the shield of Sir Lancelot of the Lake and shouted with joy.

By then Sir Lancelot was stepping down from the cart and crying out loudly, so that the whole castle rang with his words, 'Show yourself, false traitor. It is I, Sir Lancelot, come to put you to the sword!'

When the cowardly Sir Meliagaunt heard those words, he ran quickly to the queen and fell to his knees, begging for mercy.

'I beg of you, madam, tell Lancelot not to kill me.

67

What I did was out of love for you. I promise never to harm you again. You shall all be free to return to Camelot tomorrow.'

Thereupon, the queen went forth to greet her champion, led him into the castle and commanded him to cause no more bloodshed.

'I thank you most heartily for coming to our rescue,' she said. 'But the traitor knight repents his sin and wishes to make amends.'

Sir Lancelot was loath to disobey the queen, so he reluctantly agreed to spare Sir Meliagaunt, but not until he had accepted a challenge to joust at Camelot a week from then.

Meanwhile, Guinevere led Lancelot to her chamber where she dressed his wounds, just as she had done for all her other knights.

At suppertime, every man and woman from King Arthur's court was treated most graciously, the wounded given salves to heal their wounds, and all provided with good food and wine, each according to their needs. When the company was tired, they were taken to fine chambers where they slept the night.

Early next morning, King Arthur arrived with an armed company of knights, and when Queen Guinevere told him what had passed, he was relieved: but he only agreed to spare the traitor's life when he learned of the planned duel.

'Honour shall be satisfied according to our vows,' he said.

A week later, the joust was held at noon.

Both knights, Sir Lancelot and Sir Meliagaunt, set to their lance and shield and rode towards the other: they met with such force that both men were knocked breathless to the ground. But at once they were on their feet and striking at each other with their heavy swords. Such was their fury that both shields were soon broken and their helmets smashed; thick red blood stained their clothes and mingled with the mud. Finally, Sir Lancelot, seeing his opponent weakening, redoubled his efforts and, with one mighty blow, forced Meliagaunt to his knees.

Meliagaunt cried out for all to hear, 'Most noble knight, I yield to you. As Knight of the Round Table, you are duty-bound to show mercy and spare my life.'

Sir Lancelot would not break his knightly vow, yet he was determined to avenge the queen's honour to the death. So he bade Meliagaunt continue the battle; but the traitor cowered on the ground.

'You may rearm yourself,' said Lancelot, 'while I fight without my helmet and with one hand tied behind my back.'

At once the cowardly knight leapt to his feet and donned new armour, while Sir Lancelot had one hand bound behind him. Then he came rushing at Lancelot poised to strike at his unprotected head; but Sir Lancelot swiftly moved aside giving his opponent such a buffeting with his sword that it cleaved his head in two.

Thus the queen's honour was avenged.

It was not long after the joust that the ill-meaning knight Sir Mordred began to spread rumours about Queen Guinevere and Sir Lancelot. 'How can King Arthur put up with another man's love for his wife? Why is it that everyone but the king can see what is going on? It is shameful to see how Lancelot carries on behind the king's back. Everyone knows what happened between him and Guinevere at Meliagaunt's castle. '

King Arthur grew red with anger at these words. Turning on Mordred, he cried, 'If what you say is true and they are guilty, they must be brought to trial. Have the court assemble to pass judgement.'

Such was the law that no matter who was found guilty of treason, of whatever rank, the only verdict could be death—by burning at the stake. And to betray the king was the highest treason of all!

Sir Lancelot was away on a quest, but when Queen Guinevere was asked directly whether she loved Lancelot or the king, she could not deny the truth: 'I love my lord King Arthur dearly, and I have never betrayed that love. But, before God, I will not deny my love also for Sir Lancelot.'

That last confession sealed her fate.

Early next morning, the queen was led from the castle dressed in a plain white smock. She was taken to a stake in the courtyard, bound securely and had brushwood strewn about her feet.

Yet as the torch was being lit, a shout rent the air as Sir Lancelot came charging through the castle gates. With his sword flashing to right and left, he cut a swathe through the crowd guarding the queen, then slashed through Guinevere's ropes and swept her up on to his horse.

Before anyone could stop him, he had raced off into the forest, making for his castle, Joyous Guard, in the hills of North Wales.

King Arthur was mad with rage. He quickly gathered an army and pursued the fugitives all the way to Lancelot's castle; and there he laid siege to it. King Arthur shouted, 'Come out and fight, you coward! You have stolen my wife and brought shame on our brotherhood.'

From the ramparts came a cry. 'I will not fight the noblest king that ever lived. Queen Guinevere is as loyal to you as the truest lady to her man. Anyone who says otherwise is the basest villain alive! My lord, let us make peace. You have let a false knight sow strife between us.'

King Arthur was moved by his words, and he watched uncertainly as Lancelot emerged from the castle gates, followed by Queen Guinevere. With tears flowing down his cheeks, Sir Lancelot bowed before the queen and kissed her hand. Then he mounted his horse and rode away into exile.

And his going signalled an end to the fellowship of the knights.

8

The Death of King Arthur

After Lancelot's departure, Arthur had to deal with rising discontent among his earls and barons. No sooner had he doused the flames of one fire in his far-flung realm than another flared up at the other end. And then another and another.

Some knights favoured Sir Lancelot, believing that Arthur's ageing fellowship was now too weak to rule. Others blamed the king for his unjust treatment of Queen Guinevere and for heeding Mordred's slander. Many were keen to take advantage of unrest to expand their estates.

It was not long before Arthur's realm was split apart by civil war; there was now hatred where love and trust had been before.

By this time Arthur's power reached far across the sea; but revolt was rising there as well. So now he had to prepare an army to put down the malcontents in Gaul. But who was to rule while he was gone?

Lancelot was in exile, God knew where; the trusty Sir Gawain was recovering from battle wounds; and many, like the king's steward Sir Kay, were no longer youthful men. In any case, Arthur had become distrustful of all but a few of his closest knights. In the end, the king decided on a member of his own family.

Now, Arthur had always felt some guilt for the death of Morgana's father—despite the trouble she had caused. And he had made her son, Sir Mordred, his close adviser, even believing his assurance of Guinevere's betrayal. So it was to Mordred he turned to rule while he was away.

Mordred was an ambitious man who had bided his time at King Arthur's court, doing all he could to curry favour with the king. But as soon as Arthur had left Britain with his knights, he saw his chance to seize power: he summoned all the high-ranking barons of the land, lavished gifts upon them and flattered them with promises of new conquests and land. But his treason did not end there.

He produced a false letter with King Arthur's seal, and read it out to an assembly of barons. This is what he claimed King Arthur said:

> 'My Dear Nephew, Beloved Mordred, I lie mortally wounded, struck down by that traitor Lancelot; all my men have been killed. It is now that I feel more love for you than for any other because of the great loyalty you have shown. Therefore, I appoint you king in my place. My dying wish is that you marry my queen; if you do not, Lancelot is bound to attack and take her as his wife.
>
> Your loving Uncle,
> ARTHUR'

When he had finished reading, Mordred pretended to be beside himself with grief. All through the castle people grieved so loudly that you would not have heard God thundering in the heavens. And when the news spread that the king and his army had been destroyed, poor and rich lamented—for he was the most loved of all the kings in the world. The mourning lasted a week, and the common people grieved most of all.

Once the mourning ended, however, Mordred went to the most powerful of the barons and asked them about the king's last testament. The barons debated long and hard before deciding to crown Mordred king, to make the widowed queen his wife, and to swear allegiance to him. Mordred seemed to be their best hope of keeping the peace. Did not Arthur state that as his dying wish?

'Since you are all agreed,' said Mordred on hearing their decision, 'I will tell the archbishop to perform the wedding ceremony.'

Yet when the knights went to fetch the queen, she rejected their demand, saying she would rather die than wed another man. 'I could never have such a noble husband as King Arthur,' she said firmly.

But the knights persisted. 'My lady, you cannot refuse; you are duty bound to do as we command.'

Of course, they were right: she had no power now that the king was gone. But she made up her mind to escape and find refuge where the evil Mordred would not reach her; so she told the knights, 'Give me time to consider. I will grant you my reply tomorrow at noon.'

When the party had left, Guinevere locked herself in her room, crying and wringing her hands. What was she to do? After several hours, she sent her maid for the only knight she could trust—her cousin Sir Labor. When she was alone with him, she asked his advice.

'My lady,' he said, moved by her misery, 'I shall arrange your escape, to the convent abbey at Almesbury where the abbess will give you refuge. Even the godless Mordred will not dare defile a holy place.

'You should send a message to Sir Lancelot. When he learns of this treachery he will come immediately. Moreover, if King Arthur is alive—for I do not think that he is dead—a messenger will find him in Gaul and he will return with his men and slay Sir Mordred, this traitor knight.'

Guinevere readily agreed to this plan and in the dead of night she made her way to Almesbury. And when next day Mordred and his barons went to hear the queen's reply, they were furious to find her gone.

Mordred commanded his men to track down the fleeing queen. It was not long before she was traced to the convent and Mordred descended on the abbey with his army. Yet despite his dire threats, the abbess refused to hand over the queen. And Guinevere herself cried out, 'I would rather die by my own hand than marry you.'

Hearing of the siege, the aged archbishop came and warned Sir Mordred, 'Do you not fear God's vengeance? How dare you defile His sanctuary. You do great harm to the queen and all this land.'

That only inflamed Mordred even more.

'Silence, you false priest,' he shouted, 'or you will lose your head!'

But the old man was not cowed by the pretender king.

'If you do not leave, I'll damn you with bell, book, and candle!'

Mordred would have run the archbishop through there and then had not his barons intervened—and the archbishop fled to Glastonbury where he became a hermit priest, saying prayers for King Arthur.

All the same, Sir Mordred did return to Camelot; there

were more pressing matters to confront. He alone in Britain knew he had to prepare an army for Arthur's return.

Meanwhile, Queen Guinevere had sent a messenger to seek Arthur in Gaul, should he still be alive; and Arthur soon learned that Mordred had had himself crowned king, and that Sir Mordred was intending to make the queen his wife. There and then Arthur made a solemn vow:

'Mordred, you traitor, I shall let the whole world know your treachery. God forbid that you should die by anyone's hand but mine!'

Forthwith, Arthur instructed his army to be ready to leave at dawn: they were returning home to deal with Mordred.

In the morning, as soon as it was light, the tents and pavilions were taken down, and horse-drawn biers were made to bear the wounded home. They rode hard until they reached the coast of Gaul and prepared to cross the sea in a fleet of galleys.

Now, Sir Mordred had worked hard to court the barons—he granted them such costly gifts that many threw in their lot with him. Even when news came that the king's army was about to land, many disloyal barons pledged Mordred their support.

Although Arthur had always been a good and just king, bringing peace and order to his land, many now forgot his virtues. He who was the noblest king of all, lord of the greatest fellowship of knights to whom all Britain owed her glory, was now so easily cast out. Mordred had spread rumours, claiming that Arthur had brought only war and strife, while he, Mordred, would bring peace and plenty to the realm.

Thus, when Arthur arrived at Dover, there was Sir

Mordred's army waiting for him on the shore; and even before Arthur's men could make dry land, Mordred launched ships full of men-at-arms.

There was much slaughter of gentle knights on both sides. But Arthur was so brave and daring that no host of knights could prevent him landing, and he finally gained the shore with most of his men, putting Mordred to flight.

At the news of King Arthur's victory, many men flocked to his standard. It was agreed that one last decisive battle between the two armies was to be fought upon the Monday after Trinity. The battlefield would be the plain of Camlann in the Vale of Avalon.

Arthur could hardly wait to take revenge upon his treacherous foe.

As the appointed day approached, King Arthur had the strangest dream: he dreamed that a lady came to him, the most beautiful he had ever seen. She lifted him up and took him through the air to the highest mountain he had ever seen. There she placed him on a wheel full of seats, some rising, some falling. His seat was at the very top of the wheel.

'This is life's wheel of fortune,' she said. 'Tell me what you can see.'

'The entire world,' said Arthur, straining his eyes.

'There is little of the world beyond your rule,' she said. 'You have been the most powerful king that ever was. But such is mortal pride that no one sits so high that he can avoid a fall.'

Then she shook him hard and pushed him off his seat, so that he fell all the way to the ground, landing in a heap. It seemed he had broken every bone in his body.

Then he woke up. At once he summoned Sir Lucan and Sir Belvedere, telling them of his dream.

'This is an omen. We must make a treaty with Sir Mordred; offer him lands and trophies as you think fit. At all costs we must call a truce—for my dream is a warning of my death and Britain's fall should battle commence.'

Lucan and Belvedere went to Sir Mordred, encamped with a vast host on Camlann plain. For long they bargained and at last Mordred consented to take Cornwall and Kent right away, and all of Britain after Arthur's death. To seal the truce a meeting was arranged between Sir Mordred and King Arthur midway between the two hosts.

On the eve of the meeting, King Arthur went for a ride on his horse with the archbishop who had joined him from his hermit chapel. As they rode into the hills above the plain of Camlann, they came to a rock with a worn inscription carved into it. As Arthur made out the words in the fading light, he read:

BELOW THIS ROCK A MIGHTY BATTLE
WILL ORPHAN BRITAIN

'My lord,' said the archbishop, 'Merlin himself wrote those words, and there was truth in all he said—he alone knew what was to come. If you fight Mordred, your people will be orphaned by your death.'

But Arthur merely laughed.

'Well, for once Merlin was wrong. There will be no battle since I intend to sign a treaty of peace; it is all agreed.'

The archbishop was silent as the two men returned to camp. Early in the morning of that fateful day, the Monday after Trinity, two bands of fourteen men rode out to sign the truce: one was headed by King Arthur attended by Sir Lucan; the other was headed by Sir Mordred attended by King Lot of Lothian.

It was an uneasy moment. Both men had every reason to suspect treachery from the other, and their attendants kept a nervous hand on their sword hilts. The ranks of knights and men-at-arms watched silently as Arthur and Mordred dismounted and embraced. Every soldier held his breath, wary of trickery.

Before riding out, King Arthur had warned his men to start the battle at the first sign of a drawn sword; Mordred had done likewise.

No one suspected the tragic twist of fate.

As Arthur went to dismount, his horse disturbed an adder curled up in the long heath grass. Before it could strike, Sir Lucan drew his sword and cut off its head—without giving it a thought.

But when the two armies saw the flashing steel, the sunlight gleaming on the naked sword, they thought that treachery was afoot.

The white flags came fluttering down, trumpets sounded the alarm, horns blew, drums rolled and knights prepared to charge. Nothing could stop the battle now.

As Arthur rode back to his men, he gave a despairing cry, 'All Britain will regret this fateful day!'

Indeed, there was never a crueller battle in any Christian land. Nor was a field soaked in so much blood.

The battle raged all day. The armies were engaged in such close contact that longbows and lances were of no use at all; men fought toe to toe with swords and knives. And no man gave ground until a fatal wound laid him low. Arthur was everywhere on the battlefield, rallying, inspiring, leading his men.

But as dusk fell, hardly a man remained alive on the crowded field. Arthur could find only two of his good knights, Lucan and his brother Belvedere—and they were bleeding badly from their wounds. Across the bloodstained corpses, however, he suddenly caught sight of the traitor Mordred rising from the ground.

Now was his chance to kill the man responsible for this misery. Snatching up a lance, he went to rush at his foe; but Lucan tried to stop him.

'Lord, he is more miserable alive than dead. Wait, remember your dream: if you get through this day alive, your time will come again and you can slay him later.'

But Arthur was blinded by fury. With lance raised he rushed at Mordred across the bloody ground. As he ran, his scabbard came loose and fell to the ground with Excalibur; such was Arthur's rage that he did not even notice the loss.

'Traitor, your end has come!' he cried.

On hearing that shout, Mordred glanced up and raised his sword to defend himself. Too late. Arthur ran him through with such force that half the lance came out the other side. Some say that when Arthur wrenched out the lance, a ray of bright sunlight passed right through the wound.

Yet as Mordred pitched forward on his face, his sword came down on Arthur's head and bit into his skull.

Mordred now lay dead upon the ground with Arthur across him.

Lucan and Belvedere rushed to Arthur's aid and carried him to a little chapel beside the nearby lake. The effort was too much for the wounded Lucan: he collapsed and died inside the door, his guts spilled out upon the floor. Now only Belvedere remained; and he wept over his slain king.

But Arthur was not dead. After a while his eyes opened and he murmured, 'Do not weep, noble Belvedere.

I have duties to perform before I die. Listen closely and heed my words. Fetch my sword and scabbard, take them to the lakeside and throw them out into the lake. Then come straight back and tell me what you have seen.'

'My lord,' said Belvedere, 'it shall be done at once.'

However, on the way down to the lake with the sword and scabbard, Sir Belvedere gazed at the noble blade, its hilt glittering with precious gems, its scabbard gleaming in the sun. And he thought to himself, if I cast this rich sword away, it will be lost for ever.

So he hid Excalibur beneath a tree and hastened back to Arthur, claiming the deed was done.

'And what did you see?' asked the king.

'Why, nothing, sire,' he said, 'nothing but waves upon the swell.'

'You tell me false,' said Arthur with a sigh. 'Go, do as I ask; if I am at all dear to you, spare not the sword and throw it into the water.'

So Belvedere returned once more to the lake with the sword in his hand; yet again he thought it a shame to cast away such a noble blade. And he hid it beneath a gorse bush before returning to King Arthur and swearing that the deed was done.

'And what did you see?' asked Arthur.

'Nothing, sire, save lapping waters and scudding waves.'

'You have betrayed me twice,' said Arthur weakly. 'Who would have thought that you, a noble knight and loyal friend, would now betray me on my deathbed! Go again, quickly, for my time is fast running out. Already I feel death's chill hand upon my breast.'

Sir Belvedere was deeply ashamed. He took the sword and ran with it to the lake; there he swung it by the hilt and flung it with the scabbard as far as he could. And as it was flying through the air, there came an arm out of the lake to catch the sword before it touched the water. Three times the white-clad arm brandished the sword in the air and then vanished beneath the waters of the lake.

When Belvedere told the king what had happened, a smile passed over Arthur's face and he asked the knight to help him to the water's edge. As Belvedere did so, a black barge suddenly came gliding through the mist, carrying three women wearing crowns; they were sobbing as if their hearts would break.

As the barge drew in to shore, the three queens carried Arthur to the barge and laid him in the prow.

'Oh, Arthur,' said one—it was Nimue, Lady of the Lake, 'why did you wait so long? Alas, you have already lost much blood.'

As Belvedere watched, the black barge moved slowly from the bank, and he cried out, 'Sire, what is to become of us?'

'Comfort yourself as best you can,' came Arthur's voice across the waves. 'As for me, I go now into the Vale of Avalon to have my wound tended. Pray for my soul and bear these words to the remaining knights: I shall come again when Britain needs me most; then the land will rise once more out of the gloom.'

The black barge sailed off into the mists of time. The lapping of the waves, the sighing of the wind, and the weeping of the queens all merged into a song so mournful, it broke the hearts of all who heard it.

When news of King Arthur's fate reached the abbey at Almesbury, Queen Guinevere donned black robes and took a nun's vows; henceforth she passed her days in prayer, fasting, and granting alms. No one could comfort her in her misery.

Meanwhile, far away in the city of Gaunes, a messenger finally found Sir Lancelot, bringing him news of Mordred's treachery and Guinevere's distress. He left at once for Britain and, on arrival in Dover, learned the story of Arthur's last fight, of Mordred's death, and Guinevere's holy vows.

He was too late.

He rode alone to the abbey at Almesbury and sought shelter for the night. The abbess received him politely and granted him refuge in a monk's cell; yet as she led him through the cloisters they passed a nun who, on seeing Sir Lancelot, gave a strangled cry and fell down in a faint. When Sir Lancelot knelt beside her, he saw that it was Guinevere. She was carried to the convent hall and left alone with the grieving knight.

As she opened her eyes and recognized her beloved knight, she murmured sadly, 'Dear Lancelot, I beg of you, for all the love that was between us, never look upon my face again. Leave me forever. For as well as I loved you, my heart will not permit me to see you again. All I ask is for you to remember me now and then and pray that we may be forgiven.'

'Dear Guinevere,' he said, tears in his eyes, 'I cannot be false to my vow to love you for ever. I shall follow the same path as you have taken, and spend my days in prayer. Before I leave, pray kiss me one last time.'

But Guinevere refused to break her vow. And they parted. There never was a man or woman so hard-hearted as would not have wept to see the pain and sorrow between them.

Lancelot rode all day and night through a dark, dense

forest so that none should see his tears. And he began to live as a hermit in the Black Chapel deep within a forest near Glastonbury. One night, some twelve months hence, he had a dream in which he was summoned back to Almesbury.

'By the time you get there,' the vision said, 'you will find poor Guinevere dead.'

As soon as he awoke, Lancelot hurried to Almesbury where the abbess met him at the convent gates.

'My noble lord,' she said, 'I have grievous news: our sister Guinevere died just half an hour ago; she had lost the will to live. But I have a message for you.'

Lancelot wept openly as he read,

'Dear Lancelot,

I pray that I may not live to see you again. It is through our love that the lion of Britain is dead. Please take my body and bury it beside the lake at Avalon. I shall be truer to Arthur in death than I was in life.

Guinevere'

The abbess led Lancelot to Guinevere's pale cold body; he kissed her once upon the brow. After a moment's silence, he ordered an open coffin to be prepared for her and placed upon a horse-drawn bier. Then, with a hundred torches burning all about her, he led the funeral procession, singing hymns and saying prayers, all the way to Camlann. And when they came to the chapel by the lake, he had her body wrapped thirty times in waxed cloth and laid to rest in a lead coffin within a marble tomb.

When everyone had gone, Sir Lancelot lay upon the tomb for several days; then he made his way back to his hermitage where he ceased to eat or drink. He soon wasted right away, suffering cold, hunger, and thirst; and his wits were scattered to the winds. Though many went in search of him, none recognized the half-naked, wild creature as the once handsome Sir Lancelot.

His last tormented dream was of himself standing between a smiling Guinevere and Arthur, joining their hands together and pledging them eternal rest. When Sir Belvedere finally found his body, he was surprised to see a happy, peaceful smile upon his lips.

After he was buried, these words were written on his tomb:

HERE LIES SIR LANCELOT
THE BEST OF ALL KING ARTHUR'S KNIGHTS

Epilogue

The glory of King Arthur's knights of the Round Table passed into history. Soon after Arthur's death, the Saxons conquered the whole of Britain and the dark ages descended.

And yet the story of King Arthur was never forgotten. People kept faith with his promise that one day he would return—when his land was in greatest danger. Had he not pledged to lead Britain out of the gloom?

Some say he is sleeping in a cave somewhere in the Vale of Avalon. There is a story told of a shepherd who once wandered into a valley in search of lost sheep. As he climbed a hill and peered over the ridge, he found himself gazing down into a lake.

Was it the wind playing tricks with his ears, or did he really hear muffled sounds coming from a cave beside the lake?

He was about to hurry off when, to his surprise, he noticed a woman dressed in a pale blue robe with a girdle of gold about her waist. She was standing on the bank, staring at him.

'Welcome to the Vale of Avalon,' she said.

Her words were like aspen leaves trembling on the breeze.

'I am Nimue, Lady of the Lake. Tell them the time is almost come.'

With that she was gone.

Whatever did she mean?

He had no time to wonder, for all at once he saw a strange old man hobbling towards him, pointing a trembling, deathly-white finger.

'Shhhsssss,' he hissed—his voice was like dead leaves crackling underfoot. 'Do not wake them.'

'Wake whom?' the shepherd asked.

The old man seemed to shake rime and dust from his straggly hair before staring wildly about. He then repeated gruffly, 'Shhhsss! The time is not yet come.'

'But Nimue said to tell you it is almost come,' the shepherd said.

The old greybeard stared all around. 'So it is true,' he muttered.

The shepherd suddenly understood.

'You must be Merlin,' he exclaimed. 'Merlin the magician, King Arthur's bard!'

At that moment he heard a gurgling and gushing of water: a fountain had spurted from the foothills and was now pouring out its waters; they were swirling down into the lake.

Merlin leaned forward and drank freely, bathing his temples in the ice-cold stream.

'You see,' he said without glancing up, 'after King Arthur's last battle he was brought here to the Lake of

Avalon. The Lady of the Lake is skilled in the healing arts and she cured his wounds with magic herbs.

'Arthur vowed to rise again in his country's darkest hour, when he was needed most. And now the time is almost come . . .'

Merlin beckoned the shepherd to follow him into the cave beside the lake; the wizard lit torches round the walls, and flickering light fell on a whole host of sleeping men—some in armour, some with quivers of arrows, some with swords and lances. In the centre, asleep on high wooden chairs, were two figures wearing crowns.

One was a handsome bearded man with a careworn face; the other was a beautiful woman, tears glistening on her pallid cheeks.

'That is King Arthur and Queen Guinevere,' whispered Merlin. 'She weeps because she thinks her husband is dead; he grieves for his country's fate.' Pointing into the shadowy depths of the cave, Merlin then said, 'Go quickly, sound the bell!'

Following Merlin's gaze, the shepherd saw in the shadows a big brass bell. Tiptoeing towards the bell, he nervously struck both sides. The clanging echoed round the rocky walls, loud enough to wake the dead.

At once, bodies stirred, stretched, stood up; and voices from all corners called, 'Is it time? Is it time?'

'The time is almost come,' said Merlin.

King Arthur awoke his wife with a kiss upon her tear-stained cheek, and Guinevere, eyes now smiling, gazed about her, searching for Sir Lancelot, Sir Lucan, Sir Gawain, and other knights.

While the men polished their rusty swords and armour, the shepherd followed Merlin and Arthur out of the cave down to the lakeside; they seemed to know what to expect. As Arthur gazed across the still blue waters, a slender arm appeared, holding aloft a shining sword. The sword moved above the waves, like a heron swooping low across the lake, and came right to the bank.

As Arthur took it, he waved Excalibur high above his head, summoning his army from the cave. With Guinevere and Merlin at his side, he addressed them all.

'Good, noble knights. The time is nigh. Soon our people will call us and we shall go forth to restore glory to this once-great land.'

A mighty roar rent the air as the knights raised their swords and lances high into the air. And with King Arthur at their head, they marched away to do battle for their country's honour.